MIRROR-WALKER II
The Rescue Of Beloved

Mitchell Micone

MIRROR-WALKER II
The Rescue Of Beloved

Fiction4All

Chapter One
"Chi in the Morning"

Detective Robert Nash sang softly to himself as he stepped out of the shower. He was moving more slowly than usual because his morning routine– including a long, hot shower– was the most relaxing part of his day. He treasured his morning time because it prepared him for a possible day of stress and danger chasing criminals, or an equally possible long and boring day on a stakeout, or even worse– and just as possible– a day trapped in the office doing paperwork. All three scenarios were realities of being a police detective in a small Iowa town.

Dripping water on the large bath mat and still singing softly to himself, he stepped over in front of the sink and picked up a can of shaving cream. He squirted some out onto his fingers and had just reached up to smear the lather across his chin when a face suddenly appeared in the mirror.

For just an instant, his own face with its disheveled hair and shadow of a beard was replaced by the face of a young Chinese girl. She was screaming and appeared almost hysterical. Robert jumped back from the mirror and yelled, "What the hell!?!"

When he looked back into the mirror, his own image stared back at him.

"Flashbacks," he said to himself, shaking his shoulders. Then he added, "Or maybe I'm going to have to check with David to see if anything is going on."

He again raised his hand to put the shaving cream on his face. This time he didn't jump or cry out when the screaming face again appeared in the mirror. Instead, he looked around the room as if looking for someone and said, "Chi? Are you here? What's going on?"

He looked back into the mirror. Again, the face

flashed for just an instant. This time the girl wasn't crying or screaming. Instead, she was looking at him with very wide eyes as if she were pleading with him to act.

"Chi," he said loudly. "I don't know what is going on, but I understand that you are here trying to contact me and that something must be terribly wrong." He paused as if thinking quickly and then said, "Give me thirty minutes and then come to me again. I will be in my office by then. I'll make sure there is a mirror near me."

He looked around the room almost frantically. "Chi, I can't hear you or see you except for that brief instant when you are first coming through the mirror. If you understand what I asked you to do, go back and come through the mirror again, but this time, smile so I know you understand what I asked you to do."

He then turned and stared into the mirror. Almost immediately, the face once again flashed in front of him. This time the face which he saw for only an instant was smiling– or at least her mouth was almost formed in a smile. It was more like a grimace. Tears were brimming in her eyes, but it was obvious that she was trying to force a smile.

"OK!" Robert yelled. "Come back to me in thirty minutes and I'll have a plan so we can talk."

He stared into the mirror for a minute or two making sure that the face was not reappearing, then he ran to his bedroom and grabbed his phone out of its charger. His first call was to the dispatcher. "Helen," he said quickly, "it's me, Detective Nash. I need you to send a car over to David Malone's house."

He listened for a moment and then added, "Tell them it's a wellness check with suspicions of foul play. If there is no answer, break in if they have to. It might be a crime scene so tell them to be careful."

After a pause, he said thoughtfully, "You better send two cars. If something hinky is going on it might be best to have backup already there and standing by."

He again listened for a moment and then pressed a button to clear the call. His second call was to a service that he had to use occasionally. "This is Detective Robert Nash of the Plain City, Iowa, Police Department," he began. "I have need of a telephone interpreter for Mandarin Chinese. I will call back in approximately thirty minutes." He shook his head up and down as he listened to the response. "Got it," he finally said. Then he added, "Yes, Inspector Harris will authorize the standard rate."

Setting his phone back on the dresser, Robert raced back into the bathroom and hurriedly shaved, dried himself, and combed his hair. This morning was no longer a time for leisure and relaxation. Racing back into the bedroom, he hurriedly dressed and headed for the door. The only thing that slowed him down was the fact that in his haste, he keyed the wrong code into his gun safe and had to re-enter it several times in order to get to his service weapon.

Twenty minutes later he was walking quickly into the squad room at police headquarters. A framed mirror was tucked under his arm. Inspector Harris was standing next to his desk waiting for him.

"What in the hell do you need a Mandarin Chinese translator for?" he yelled as Robert approached. "And why did you send two patrol cars to David Malone's house?"

"I don't have time to explain right now," the detective replied. "And you wouldn't believe me anyway. Just let this play out and I'll explain later."

"Do you have any idea what these translators cost us?" the inspector yelled. He was almost screaming now and his nose was nearly touching Robert's.

Detective Nash pulled away from him and drew himself up to his full six-foot three height. Then he smiled at his boss and said in his best imitation of Clark Gable, "Frankly, my dear, I don't give a damn."

His face then turned very serious as he said quickly, "If I'm wrong, I'll pay the fee myself. ... But if I'm right, David Malone is in really deep trouble."

"You can get away with an awful lot if you're right," the inspector said firmly. Then he added harshly, "Just don't ever be wrong."

"Yes, sir," Robert snapped back as he set the mirror on his chair and pulled the phone into the center of his desk. He picked up a pad of paper from the corner of his desk and wrote something across it before setting it next to the telephone.

"Chi, if you're already here," he said as if talking to the mirror, "just wait a little bit. I said a half hour and it's only been twenty-five minutes."

"Who in the hell are you talking to?" demanded Inspector Harris.

"Patience," Robert answered. "Patience."

For the next five minutes he paced back and forth in front of his desk. Then, he stood in front of his desk and faced the mirror. "I have no idea where you are in the room," he said, "but I am assuming that you are here and you can understand me. David said that you can read American numbers, so I wrote my direct line phone number on that pad on my desk. What I want you to do is wait ten more minutes..." He turned and pointed to a clock on the wall. "That would be nine fifteen our time. Then call that number. Just say anything so I know that you are there and I will bring a translator onto the line who can tell me what you are saying."

"This is bullshit!" Inspector Harris said loudly. "I'm pulling the plug on this nonsense right now!"

"You'd better take the call on line two before you

do that," a voice said from behind him. One of the desk clerks from the main area was standing in the doorway. She looked upset, like she wasn't sure what she was supposed to do. Her hands were bouncing slightly as she held her arms at her sides.

"Who's it from?" the inspector asked quickly.

"The White House," she answered in a shaky voice. "It's the First Lady and she said she needed to talk to you before you did something stupid."

"I made a few calls on my way in," Detective Nash said with a suppressed smile. "I have a feeling this is a lot bigger than it looks."

Inspector Harris' face was pale, but impassive, as he said softly, "I'll take the call at my desk."

Before turning to walk into his office, he said brusquely to Detective Nash, "You'd better be right about this."

"I wish I wasn't," Robert responded, "but I'm afraid I am."

A few moments later, Inspector Harris returned to the squad room. "She wants this on speaker," he said glumly as he pushed a button on Robert's phone and motioned for someone to close the door.

"You are on speaker now," Inspector Harris said loudly.

"Thank you," came a voice from the speaker. "For those of you who don't know who I am, I am Helena Travis, wife of President Douglas Travis. The details of David Malone's involvement in my rescue last year have been kept from the public, but let me assure you that without his help I would never have been found... at least not alive."

She paused slightly and then said more loudly and firmly, "And when I was found, Mister Malone put his body between me and a gunman who was about to shoot me." After another short pause she said with some emotion in her voice, "That is why this is important to me."

A male voice came through the speaker, "And the reason that it is important to me is that he stopped a very complex plot to create a war between us and China." There was a slight cough. "He nearly single-handedly stopped that plot, but the people behind it were never caught. We believe this might be a first move by those bastards to take David out of the picture before they try something new. This has to be kept out of the public eye as much as possible, but you will have my full support for whatever you need."

"Yes, sir, Mister President," Inspector Harris snapped back, almost standing at attention as he spoke.

"And one more thing," the President said, "you can't be sure of anyone in this. The last time, the head of the Secret Service was involved. All communication comes through Helena... actually through Mark Nash, her personal bodyguard. You got that?"

A chorus of "Yes, Mister President," rang out in the room.

"OK, then," he answered brusquely. "Keep us informed. ... and find that kid."

The line was dead before the second chorus of "Yes, Mister President" filled the room.

Inspector Harris looked across the desk at Detective Nash for several seconds before releasing a deep breath and saying, "Your request for a translator is approved."

"I don't think that will be necessary," said a voice from the doorway. Everyone looked up to see the same desk clerk who had announced the call from the White House peeking around the door. She looked just as disturbed and upset as she did when she had talked to the White House.

"Your phone was busy," she said, "so the call

10

transferred over to me. A woman named Kong Ling, from Penglai, Shandong, China, wants to speak to the man her granddaughter calls Warrior Robert.

"That would be me," Detective Nash said slowly. After a pause, he asked, "Is she speaking English?"

"I don't speak Chinese," the clerk responded as she shrugged her shoulders and turned to walk away.

"Put it through," Robert called out after her.

Chapter Two
"Momma Ling"

To say that everyone in the squad room was listening attentively to the incoming phone call would be a vast understatement. All work had stopped and the five officers present were staring intently at the phone.

"Listen up, all of you," Inspector Harris yelled as he turned slowly around to look at the three men and one woman under his command. "I need you to hear this so you know what is going down, but if I hear that any one of you has breathed a word of this to anyone– and I mean anyone– I will personally shoot you and rely on getting a presidential pardon for doing it." He paused a moment before saying gruffly, "You got that!?"

Robert nodded. Two of the other officers shouted back "Yes, sir!" Sergeant Garcia, who often worked undercover yelled, "Damn straight!"

Her voice could be heard clearly over the others, but the inspector didn't seem to notice because a voice almost immediately came from the phone saying, "Am I speaking to the man my granddaughter calls 'Warrior Robert?'"

"That would be me," Robert replied. "My name is Detective Robert Nash. Your granddaughter Chi is known to me from our work together last year."

The woman on the phone laughed slightly. "Her name is actually Kong Jing. Chi was her baby name. No one calls her that anymore. She is Jing, but the mirror often changes things slightly. If she spoke of me in the mirror, it would possibly have been as 'Momma Ling', but I am properly Kong Ling and would prefer that or just Ling."

"Thank you," Robert replied. "What is Kong Jing trying to tell us?"

An excited voice speaking rapidly in Chinese

could be heard in the background. "She says," Kong Ling continued, "that Beloved has been taken."

"That would be David Malone," Robert replied.

"We have been at the house," Inspector Harris said in a measured tone, "and there are indications of a forced entry, but no sign of a struggle." He scowled at his detective before adding, "He is, however, apparently missing."

Again, there was an exchange in Chinese in the background before Ling said, "It happened last night–your night, not ours, it was morning here. They were watching a movie together in the living room when Beloved suddenly disappeared. She walked to the bedroom to see what had happened to his non-mirror self and saw four men dressed in dark clothing pulling a bag over Beloved's... I mean David's head. They picked him up and carried him out of the house and into a black van which was parked in the driveway."

Kong Ling paused as Jing excitedly told her more of the story. "She then tried to contact any of the warriors who had helped Beloved in the past but was not successful until this morning when Warrior Robert saw her come through the mirror in his water closet."

"Does Chi... I mean Jing have any idea who took David or to where?" Inspector Harris asked quickly.

After an exchange in Chinese, Ling answered, "Unfortunately, no. The faces of the men were covered. She did go into the van before it pulled away, but the inside had been covered with dark cloth, so there were no mirrored surfaces in it. She had to leave before it left the safe area."

There was another pause with voices in the background. Ling continued, "She says that she could see nothing which would identify them. The only thing that might be important is that one of the men said, 'Keep that bag on his head. The boss said he would be very upset if wonder boy here sees himself in anything shiny.'"

"That's not good," Robert said softly. "That means they know he's a Mirror-Walker."

"What?!" snapped the inspector.

Robert looked up at him and said almost angrily, "Later! I'll explain everything later."

Inspector Harris didn't look pleased, but he pressed his lips together and remained quiet as Robert said, "We have to figure out some way of getting you and Chi– I mean Jing– over here in person. I don't know how much of what happened last year Jing told you, but this might be crucial to both of our countries. And she might be our only way of finding David."

He paused and chewed at his lower lip before adding more slowly, "But we have to be careful with how we do this. If this boss, whoever he is, finds out about her, she won't be safe."

"She is already not safe," Kong Ling said sadly. "She is a Mirror-Walker."

There was an audible sigh– almost a moan– before she continued, "I have already lost two children to the mirror. It is a dangerous blessing to be able to walk in mirrors."

"Is Jing willing to come here if we can figure out a way to do this without attracting attention?" Inspector Harris asked.

"I had a standing invitation from your governor to visit his wonderful state," Kong Ling said firmly. "He visited here many times when my husband was still active in the government. He was very interested in good relations between rural Iowa and rural China and is now Ambassador to my country. He probably remembers me since I acted as interpreter for many of his visits to the rural areas, so it would be easy to get that invitation officially restated."

"There will be no problem on this end," Robert said quickly. "I'm pretty sure President Travis will do whatever necessary to help us find David and will instruct the Ambassador and whoever else to do likewise."

"Then I will speak with the embassy," Ling replied. "We must make this look like I am the one who desires to travel to your country and Jing is merely accompanying me to see America. It would also be best if this appeared to go through normal channels at your embassy."

"That makes sense," Robert replied. Inspector Harris was also nodding his head in agreement.

Ling then asked, "Is there anything else?"

"Not at this time," the detective replied. "Call or text me when you know your travel plans. Do I need to give you my cell number?"

Ling laughed. This time her laugh was soft and silvery– a real laugh, not an expression of nervousness. "No," she replied. "Kong Jing already has that. She looked around quite thoroughly while she was in your apartment. She also rode with you while you drove your car to the police station."

A voice spoke rapidly in the background in Chinese and Ling laughed again. "She says that Warrior Robert really needs to clean the rubbish out of the back seat of his car."

"Tell her I will do that," he replied. Then he added softly, "Be careful. ... And keep Chi– Jing– safe."

"I will," Momma Ling replied.

Chapter Three
"Arrival"

Even with the full authority of both the United States and Chinese governments behind the effort, bureaucracy moves only so fast and commercial jets adhere to their own schedules. It was four days later when Detective Robert Nash, accompanied by Sergeant Luciana Garcia, stood at one of the arrival gates at Des Moines International Airport watching the passengers disembark.

Normally no one would be allowed to meet an incoming passenger at the gate entrance. And definitely no one would be allowed to carry a weapon into that area. But nothing about Kong Ling's and Kong Jing's arrival was normal. Both Robert and Lucy were armed.

While the detective watched the gate, Sergeant Garcia, dressed in a tight pair of jeans which drew attention to her shapely legs and a baggy sweatshirt which hid her service weapon, stood at his back watching the arrival area behind them. Her right hand was in the pocket of the sweatshirt, but seemed to be in farther than would be expected. That was because the pocket itself had been removed and her hand was actually on the handle of the Beretta Model 92SB that was tucked into the very top of her jeans. The lightweight Beretta didn't have the stopping power of a Glock 22, but it was easier to conceal and most people didn't associate a Beretta with cops. Thus, she could use the same weapon whether she was on duty or under cover. Her feeling was that when things go south, it is best to have a weapon in your hand that you are intimately familiar with.

About a dozen people had exited the ramp when Robert suddenly stiffened. A tall Chinese woman was gliding toward him. Her walk was so smooth and precise that glide was the only way to describe it. She had the poise and bearing of a model– or an aristocrat– but was dressed in a simple outfit consisting of a loose, pale gray blouse, and matching, slightly darker, gray slacks. She wore no jewelry except small silver earrings which dangled about an inch below her ears. There was a touch of gray in her coal black hair, but her face was unlined.

Directly behind her, dressed in jeans and a pullover, was a much younger, shorter version of her whom Detective Nash immediately recognized as Chi. Chi was much less graceful in her walk and was looking around very nervously. She relaxed slightly when she spied Detective Nash, and her walk began to almost match her grandmother's as they exited the ramp.

As they approached, Robert gave a short bow of his head and said to the taller woman, "You must be Kong Ling." He turned slightly and added, "I recognize Chi... I mean Kong Jing."

When they both smiled and nodded back at him, he asked, "Did you have a pleasant flight?"

Kong Ling smiled for just a moment and then replied, "Sixteen hours in an airplane is never pleasant, but it was a good flight. There were no problems." The smile left her face and her voice became flat as she added, "... with the plane or anything else."

Robert replied, also in a flat voice, "That is good." He looked over at Jing and said, "We need to get somewhere where we can talk."

Without turning around, he reached back with his hand and tapped Sergeant Garcia's back. "Clear," she immediately said in a soft voice.

"Follow me," he said firmly as he turned around. Once they had stepped out of the gateway and into the main arrival area, he again turned to Kong Ling and said, "If you give this gentlemen your baggage tags, he will retrieve your luggage."

A baggage handler suddenly appeared alongside them. He was dressed in the standard airport baggage handler's uniform, except it looked slightly tight on his muscular frame. His stern face and wary eyes also looked slightly out of place. That was because he was not a baggage handler, but in fact an agent from the FBI's Des Moines office.

He had no idea who this was he was protecting, or why he was under cover as a baggage handler, but the orders had come from the Director of the FBI, himself, with the stern warning that if he screwed it up, he would be permanently assigned to Forgotonia, wandering the rural roads of Illinois, trying to do background checks on people applying for low-level government jobs. He forced a smile as Kong Ling handed him several baggage check tags and hurried off to retrieve their luggage.

The first shot rang out as he was pulling the second suitcase off the carousel. A gunman with two automatic pistols was walking quickly through the baggage area shooting indiscriminately at the arriving passengers. Actually, it wasn't indiscriminate. All those who fell in the first hail of bullets were women over the age of fifty and teenaged girls. He was shooting rapidly without taking time to aim precisely. None of those hit were badly wounded, but all were on the ground and could not escape.

The gunman walked carefully up to the woman lying on the ground closest to him. He was raising his right arm to put a coup de grace bullet through her head when a different, slightly lighter-sounding weapon, barked twice.

The gunman jerked as the bullets struck. He tried to turn toward his attacker, but as he turned the smaller weapon barked twice again. Two red splotches immediately appeared on his chest and he dropped limply to the ground.

The response time of airport security was impressive. They had been warned that there was possibly a "credible threat" against this arriving flight. Such reports are received all the time, but each is taken seriously.

Four heavily-armed officers in full body armor burst through the doors almost before the shocked passengers could realize what was happening. The FBI agent standing over the dead assailant set his weapon on the ground, raised his hands, and began shouting loudly, "FBI, FBI, don't shoot! Don't shoot!"

Detective Nash had begun running at the first sound of gunfire. "Move! Move! Move!" he was yelling as he swung his arms indicating the direction which Kong Ling and Kong Jing should run.

Sergeant Garcia's hand was no longer in her sweatshirt. Her weapon was in the open as she yelled out, "Police! Police! Clear the way! Clear the way!"

Startled arriving passengers and cabdrivers stared at them as they burst through the airport doors running and literally jumped into a waiting car. Their siren blaring as they left blended in with the multitude of sirens streaming into the airport in response to the attack.

"So much for a low-key entrance," Detective Nash said bitterly.

"What happened?" Kong Ling asked. Her face showed her concern.

"Someone wants you... and Chi... dead," Sergeant Garcia answered forcefully.

"That means they know who you are," the detective added. He took a deep breath and then said, "And that they think you can find and free David."

Kong Ling spoke hurriedly to Kong Jing and then said, "Jing wants to get somewhere that she can go into the mirror. Then you can explain what is happening and she will understand."

"We had hotels rooms all set up here in Des Moines," Robert said quickly, "but obviously someone knew you were coming, so that won't work. We have to assume that anything we had planned is compromised."

"Where do you want me to take you?" came a voice from the front seat. Their driver was one of the other detectives from the precinct.

"David's place," Robert immediately replied. "And if you tell anyone that's where you took us, Inspector Harris will have to wait in line to shoot you. You don't even tell *HIM* where we are. And if he doesn't like that tell him to talk to my brother."

"Understood," the officer responded.

About two hours later, Detective Nash was pulling a key out of a fake rock he had gotten from beneath the bushes at the corner of David's house. The key fit the repaired office door on the side of the house. "Wait here," he said to the women as he disappeared around the side of the house. A few moments later, the garage door opened noisily and the detective reappeared, waving for them to enter.

"He keeps a garage door opener in his office," he explained as he ushered them into the kitchen. "That way he can get in if he forgets his key, but it isn't quiet so someone can't use it to sneak in." He laughed slightly, "Too bad David didn't have a high security lock on the door between his bedroom and his office," he said as he shook his head. "Maybe it would have slowed down the men who grabbed him."

"I doubt that would have made any difference," Kong Ling said in her precise English. "These men are very ruthless... and obviously desperate." She paused before saying, "Such men are very dangerous."

"Ain't that the truth," Sergeant Garcia added as

she stepped around Kong Ling and Detective Nash to inspect the interior of the house. Her shouts of "Clear!" rang out several times as she checked each room of the house. Meanwhile Robert stood just inside the door between the kitchen and the living room, waiting silently with Kong Ling and Kong Jing as Lucy Garcia made sure of their safety.

A few minutes later she came back to the kitchen. As she approached, she held up her hand and motioned for them to stay where they were. Then she held her finger to her lips indicating that they should be quiet. Robert held up his hands and shrugged his shoulders. His wide eyes expressed his question of what was going on.

In response, the sergeant held up one finger indicating that they should wait. She then slipped outside through the back door. When she returned she said, "I'm assuming the place is bugged just in case anyone came back here. It's what I would do. I doubt they have the resources to have someone watching the place twenty four-seven or to set up a local listening post, but internet bugs would do it."

She looked around and said, "Whoever put them in was most likely lazy or in a hurry, so they would have connected them directly to David's Wi-Fi rather than a neighbor's."

She smiled and said, "I pinned his cable where it comes into the house."

When Robert and Kong Ling looked at her strangely, she explained, "If you push a straight pin through the cable just above the connector and then cut it off with a nail clipper on both sides, the signal disappears and it looks like cable failure. I got a safety pin and nail clippers out of the medicine cabinet in the bathroom. A repair person just assumes the connector went bad, so they cut if off and replace it." She gestured around herself before adding, "But in the meantime, we have a better chance that the bugs aren't working."

"But the fact they aren't working," Detective Nash replied, "will tell them that something is going on here. We have to go somewhere else soon."

Kong Ling kept up a running commentary as she translated what everyone said for her granddaughter.

Kong Jing suddenly spoke up, speaking rapidly in Chinese to her grandmother. After a short response to her granddaughter, Kong Ling said, "Kong Jing says that we can use David's house on wheels... whatever that means."

"The van!" Robert answered. His shoulder's slumped as he said, "But if they bugged the house, they probably bugged the van... or put a tracking device on it."

"I can handle that," Lucy said quickly. "Or at least, I know someone who can." She bit her lower lip for a moment before adding, "At least I can if I can come up with some money."

"David keeps five grand in a go bag in his closet," Robert said. "Don't spend it all in one place."

"Gotcha," she answered as she pulled her phone from her jeans. "Hiya, Jimmy," she said happily a few moments later. "This is Lucy."

In the quiet of the room, a male voice could be heard answering, "What do you want, cop lady?"

"I need a favor, Jimmy boy," she continued.

"You are out of favors, cop lady," he spat back. "Whatever it is will cost you." His voice suddenly got very smooth as he said, "But if you don't have any money..."

"Never happen, James," Lucy said firmly. "We're talking a five hundred dollar favor."

"I'm listening."

"I need a van debugged," she said. "Full search for

anything you can think of."

"Bring it in," the voice replied.

"Can't do that," she answered. "You have to come here and nobody can know you did this."

"That ain't no five hundred dollar favor," he said almost angrily.

"OK," she replied. "A grand, plus an additional hundred for each device you find."

"Just tell me where to come," he answered with a laugh.

Sergeant Garcia gave him the address. Then she added, "Don't park nearby and don't come to the front door."

"You know," he replied, "we could always work something out in place of the money."

"Never happen, James," she said loudly as she ended the call.

***

About a half-hour later, there was a light knock on the back door. Lucy answered it and led a rather scruffily-dressed young man through the house. He slipped a large backpack off his shoulders as they entered the garage. Twenty minutes later she returned.

"Two bugs, one cell-based tracking device, and one GPS locator," she reported. "The bugs and GPS locator are active from the van's battery. The cellphone tracking device is connected through the van's computer and activates when the van is running. I'll have Jimmy move the bugs and the GPS to the car. He can just remove the tracking device since it isn't active. If they restore the cable, the other devices will still be running and they'll think the van is still parked in the garage."

"Sounds like a plan," Robert replied.

"Might cost a little extra," Lucy said as she walked

back into the garage, "but I'll see what I can work out." Shortly after she entered the garage, a loud, "Never happen, James!" could be heard followed a few moments later by a softer, "OK, but nothing more."

Ten minutes later Sergeant Garcia led Jimmy out of the garage and back through the house. At the back door, she handed him fourteen hundred dollars in cash and then gave him a light kiss on the cheek.

He said, "That isn't what we agreed to."

She sighed deeply and leaned in once again to kiss him, this time directly on the lips. She held the kiss for several seconds and then pulled back and said, "Goodnight, James."

"Goodnight, cop lady," he replied dreamily as he turned and left.

After she closed the door, she said softly, "Amazing what you can get a young man to do for just a kiss."

The sergeant then turned and looked at Detective Nash. "You never heard– or saw– any of that," she said harshly. "And if you say anything at the squad room I will put nasty stuff in your coffee for the rest of your life."

"We all have secrets," Robert replied. He shrugged slightly as he added, "At least yours are slightly believable."

Chapter Four
"On the Road"

When the two officers returned to the living room, Kong Ling was standing with Kong Jing by her side. "Jing wants to know what our plans are," she said softly. "Before we go, I think we need to talk and she needs to listen."

Kong Ling began walking toward the kitchen. Kong Jing turned and walked toward the bedroom.

"What..." Sergeant Garcia started to ask, but Detective Nash held up his hand and said, "Later. It's too hard to explain. You'll catch on pretty fast as it's happening." With that, he followed Kong Ling into the kitchen and motioned for Lucy to follow.

Once they were all seated around the kitchen table, Robert pointed to the fourth chair and said, "I think we'll give Chi a minute or two to get here." Lucy again looked perplexed, but remained silent.

After what seemed like a very long period of silence, he spoke. Turning to Kong Ling he said, "May I call you Momma Ling. Kong in my mind brings up images of a giant gorilla climbing a building."

Ling laughed lightly and said, "Yes, you may call me Momma Ling, or just Ling." She laughed again and added, "I have seen the movie... both of them. Kong is a very old family name in China, but I understand." After another light laugh she said, "And I assume that it is more comfortable for you to call my granddaughter Chi, since that is the name you knew her by from the mirror."

"Thank you, Momma Ling." He continued, "And for the sake of things, you may call us Robert and Lucy."

Ling nodded her approval and Robert turned his attention to the empty chair. "Chi," he began, "I assume you are here and can understand me. What we know... or think we know... is that David was taken by the same group that kidnaped the First Lady last year. We don't know who that is, but they are very dangerous and they have connections in both our governments."

He paused and looked over at Ling. "We have no idea where they might have taken David, or if David is still alive."

Momma Ling pursed her lips and said, "Chi assures me that David is still alive. She said that Beloved taught her that if a person is dead, a mirror need only to be close by. The spirit of the dead person will draw the Mirror-Walker to them across the void of chaos." She took a deep breath and said, "If she cannot locate him, then David is alive."

"Ok, then," Robert said firmly. "David is alive and hidden somewhere. The key to unraveling this is to find David. And the only person who can do that is Chi. We need to get somewhere safe and let her go into the mirror looking for him. Hopefully she can tell us where he is."

"She has tried," Ling said slowly. "He must be somewhere with absolutely no mirrors." She grimaced. "As emotionally linked as Chi is to Beloved, the smallest mirror would be enough for her to step through."

She looked at the empty chair and said strongly, "Despite what you say to me, my child, I know that you love him. That love may never be able to exist anywhere but in the mirror world, but in the mirror and in your heart, you do love him."

Sergeant Garcia looked at both of them. "Kong Jing is here?" she said, pointing to the chair and then looking back up at the door to the living room. She shook her head several times and added, "But she's also in the bedroom?"

"Yup," answered Robert. "She's mirror walking in

David's special black mirror. And while she's in the mirror, she can understand everything you say even though she doesn't speak a word of English... except for some words she's picked up from the internet."

"Weird," Lucy said, shaking her head.

"You haven't even begun to see weird, Sergeant," Robert replied with a laugh.

Then he got very serious. "OK. The plan is this. We go off the grid and hide somewhere. All cellphones stay here with the batteries taken out. If you can't take out the battery, we wrap it in aluminum foil and put it in the refrigerator so no signal can get out. We don't use any credit cards and don't stay in any motels. Other than that, we make it up as we go along."

He looked around the table before asking, "Any other thoughts?"

A voice speaking Chinese answered him. Robert turned to see Chi standing in the doorway. She was wearing David's robe which hung very loosely on her small frame. The oversized robe added to her look of anguish as she repeated what she had said as she approached.

"She said," Momma Ling translated, "that she will step into nothing a thousand times if that is what it takes to find Beloved."

"I hope it won't come to that," Robert answered. "I've seen where David went when he stepped into the wrong nothing." He shuddered slightly and said, "You definitely don't want to go there."

He then stood, clapped his hands, and said, "OK! Time to go! Momma Ling, you ride up front with me. Lucy, you and Chi ride in the back.

***

Detective Nash made two stops on their way out of

town. The first was at a dilapidated-looking old house alongside a junk yard. The faded sign said, "Big Dave's Auto Salvage." It also gave an internet address to order parts.

"Stay sharp," he said to the sergeant as he stepped out of the van. Lucy moved forward so she could see out of the front windows. Her service weapon was in her hand.

About twenty minutes later, Robert returned carrying a stack of license plates and a screwdriver. He set a portion of the stack on the front seat and moved to the back of the van. A few minutes later, he re-appeared in the front as he switched that plate also.

When he finally got back into the van, he said, "Normally these would be a grand a set, plus another five hundred to the kid that hacks the DMV in whichever state to change the description of the vehicle. The plates are off wrecked cars. They still have a few months on the stickers, so they will show as good if someone runs a plate check. They aren't perfect, but if they put out a BOLO on the van, traffic cameras won't pick us up and report the van."

"Can you trust him not to turn you in?" Sergeant Garcia asked. "Once word gets around, it might be worth his while."

"Big Dave would narc me out in an instant," Robert replied, "regardless of what I promised him. But I told him we're trying to rescue David." He paused and then said in a softer voice, "David found his daughter... alive. I was the one who brought her back to him after we took down the kidnappers. It was another gang trying to muscle in on his specialized internet parts business."

He looked at Lucy and Momma Ling. "That's why he didn't charge me for the plates. That's also why he's going to see that my credit cards get used in Minneapolis, Chicago, and Cleveland over the next few days so it looks like we are headed straight for Washington on the northern route.

"Your credit cards!" Lucy started to say, but her words were lost as she was thrown back into the bed when Robert accelerated out onto the street.

The second stop was at a duplex apartment which the detective owned as an investment. He pulled the van into the alley behind the house and opened the door on a long shed which faced the alley. Lucy could see what looked like the hitch to a boat trailer just inside the door. A few minutes later he set a couple of fishing poles, a tackle box, and a small duffle bag into the van and climbed back in the driver's seat.

"There's fifteen Gs plus six very cold burner phones in the bag," he said quickly. "The phones will replace the ones we left at David's. I doubt we will actually get in any fishing, but the poles will help us blend in."

He then turned to Sergeant Garcia and asked. "How much do you have in your emergency stash?"

"What makes you think I have an emergency stash?" she answered back, trying to look surprised.

Robert just continued to look at her silently. It took about three minutes before she sighed and said, "About seven grand. I keep it at my mother's place."

"Too dangerous to go there," he replied. "They know you were with me at the airport. They might be watching the house."

"Not to worry," she replied as she reached into the bag to pull out one of the cheap cellphones.

"Hello, Momma," she said a moment later, "I need to do a little shopping." She then turned the phone back off and took out the battery.

"Pre-arranged message?" Robert asked.

"Yup," Lucy answered. "Too short to trace, and even if they tried, there are two burner phones in chargers hidden up in the attic at my aunt's house down the block. I called the first. It transfers the call to the second and the second automatically calls Momma's cellphone. No way to trace it back to this phone or where I am unless they pull both phones out of the attic."

"So," he continued, "how does she get the money to you?"

"Poor man's Swiss bank account," she answered with a grin.

When both Robert and Momma Ling looked very confused, she explained. "There's a WalMart a few blocks from Momma's house. She'll go there and do some shopping. While she's there, she will go to the service desk and use some of my stash to buy a five thousand dollar money transfer. That's the largest they'll set up as an any store pickup. We just stop at a WalMart somewhere and I go in, prove who I am, and get the money. Simple as that."

"We need to do that before we leave town," he replied firmly. "Otherwise, they will know which direction we're headed. Or worse, they can put a stop order or trace on the money transfer."

"I don't think we should do that," Lucy responded. "If they see her buy the transfer, they might hang around to watch for me. There's another WalMart the next town over. We can stop there before we head out to..." She paused with a blank expression on her face.

"Where are we going?" she asked as she looked at Robert with open eyes.

"Off the grid for a couple of days," he answered as he settled into the driver's seat. "And then further off the grid if we have to."

***

The WalMart was in a shopping center on the edge of town. Robert pulled the van into the parking lot of a Meijer's in a similar strip mall on the opposite side of the highway. "You walk across and pick up the money," he instructed Lucy. "Momma Ling and I will pick up some groceries and other necessities."

Ling spoke rapidly in Chinese and then answered, "I told Chi to stay in the van. People might remember someone who did not speak English."

"Let her come in with us," Robert replied. "There's a packing plant in this town and the clerks here are probably used to at least a dozen different languages. No one will even notice."

Chi smiled when her grandmother told her that she didn't have to hide in the van.

When they returned Lucy was waiting for them.

"Cripes!" she exclaimed as they arrived at the van with four carts laden with food. "Who are you planning to feed?"

"Some of it's clothes," Robert answered curtly as he started setting bags in the back of the van. "Ling and Chi agreed that you were one size larger than Chi. I hope you like what we bought."

He paused to look at her and said, "I know it's a lot of food, but we might have to be hiding out in places where there ain't no supermarkets." As he set the last of the bags into the van he added, "Hell, there isn't even a convenience store at our first stop, and it isn't anywhere near as primitive as where we can go if we have to."

"Where are we going?" Lucy asked.

"First off," Robert answered, "we are heading over to I-35 and straight up to Minneapolis just in case anyone sees us leave the area."

"That doesn't sound primitive," Lucy responded, "or off the grid."

"We won't be going all the way into town," he

replied with a laugh. "just to the beltway. Then we come back south on 52 to a campground in Kendallville, Iowa."

"Never heard of it," Lucy replied.

"Hard to find on a map," he continued, "and even harder to find in person. It's a true blinking plumb town."

Momma Ling looked at him in confusion. "American idiom," he said with a smile. "Blink and you are plumb through it. The town is just a bar and a half-dozen houses where the highway crosses the Upper Iowa River. Campers are usually there to trout fish or canoe on the river or hang around camp and drink."

"And you know about this because...?" Lucy asked from the back.

"Because I like to fish when I'm on vacation," he answered loudly. Then in a softer voice he added, "... and drink."

***

It took five hours of driving to reach Kendallville. Robert parked the van in one of the sites at the back of the campground where they couldn't be seen from the highway. Registration involved dropping an envelope with the proper fee into a metal box bolted to the outer wall of the bathrooms. "As long as the license number on the form matches what's on the van," he said when he returned, "they don't give a shit about real names or anything else."

He looked around at the high, rocky banks which surrounded them. "Cellphones don't work worth a crap down here," he said emphatically. "You have to drive up to the top of the valley on either side of us to get a signal." He paused, smiled, and said more softly, "We are off the grid."

"Now what?" Lucy asked.

"I round up some firewood and we cook supper," he answered. "And Chi uses the mirror in the van to go looking for David."

Chi and Momma Ling were standing together next to the van. Turning to Ling, he asked, "Does she have any idea where to look? We don't know anything except that he left in a black van."

Momma Ling translated what Robert had said and suddenly Chi began yelling excitedly.

"What's she saying? What's she saying?" Robert almost yelled.

"You reminded her about the van," Ling answered. "She has been in the van, so she can go back there even if she does not know the name of anyone in it."

Chapter Five
"The Search Begins"

When Robert returned with the firewood, Momma Ling and Chi were inside the van. Sergeant Garcia was sitting at the picnic table. As he approached, she stood and walked toward him.

"What exactly does she do?" she asked in a firm voice. "Does she just go into the mirror and pop out wherever she wants?"

"Not exactly," he replied as he sat on the bench across from her. "From what David said, they have to know the name of someone or have been there before." He sighed. "And there has to be a mirror in the same room or where it can see them or whatever." Another sigh, this one deeper, "I don't know a great deal more than that. It's weird as hell, but somehow it works."

"Are there many Mirror-Walkers?" she asked.

"Just David and Chi, as far as we know," he replied. "But Chou thought he was the last and then David thought he was alone, so who knows?"

Lucy started to ask who Chou was, but the sound of the van door opening interrupted their conversation. Momma Ling was still wearing the gray blouse and slacks she had worn on the plane. Chi was wearing the white terrycloth robe that had been one of the necessities purchased along with the groceries. If it were not for the forlorn look on her face, she might have looked like a typical teenager ready to go for a swim.

Robert waited until both were standing next to the table before asking, "Well?"

Chi began speaking immediately. It was obvious that she was upset. When she did not give her grandmother time to translate, Ling held up one hand and Chi immediately fell silent.

"She says," Ling began, "that she found the van,

but it was changed. The black cloth that covered the inside was gone so there were many shiny surfaces that allowed her to enter."

She looked over at her granddaughter and Chi again began speaking rapidly. After a moment, Ling continued, "The van is parked underground in a large car park. She does not know where. There were many other identical vans parked nearby. She tried to explore, but the safe area barely reached the entrance. She could not go beyond there to see what might be up the ramp."

"Now what?" Lucy said sharply. "We have to do something."

"Haste can be your enemy's friend," Ling said softly.

"Confucius?" Robert asked.

"Me," Ling answered with a smile, pointing to herself. "My husband and I survived many changes in China because we did not blindly rush to one side or the other. Let us prepare a meal and after we have eaten we can talk about what we might be able to do."

***

Robert built a campfire, but the meal itself was prepared by Ling and Chi on the small counter-top burners in the camper. As they sat at the picnic table to eat, Momma Ling said, "I am surprised that there are enough plates and tableware. I do not think David would have had that much company in his travels."

"Speaking as a man," Robert said, "it's more likely he has about a week's worth so he doesn't have to do dishes very often." He gave a short laugh. "Even then," he added, "he probably used paper plates."

"There were also many paper plates," Ling answered, "and many plastic utensils." She wrinkled her face slightly. "You Americans are so wasteful."

"This American is tired," Lucy said. "What are the sleeping arrangements?"

"We picked up two small tents and some sleeping bags," Robert answered. As he spoke he pointed first at himself and then at Lucy. "Momma Ling and Chi will sleep in the van. Maybe something will come to us in our sleep."

When Ling translated his remarks to her granddaughter, Chi again became very agitated. Whatever she said greatly upset her grandmother, whose voice began to take on a tone of anger. In response, Chi's voice became shrill and she stomped her foot several times as she spoke. The two argued for several minutes— sometimes rather loudly— before Ling's shoulders drooped and she became silent.

"Chi says," Ling began flatly, "that there is a way to reach David even if there is not a mirror... but I will not allow it!"

"Why not?" asked Lucy.

"If a Mirror-Walker is trapped in the chaos between the mirror worlds," Ling explained, "he or she is doomed. I lost my daughter to the mirror, but I lost my son to the place of chaos."

She paused to cry silently before continuing. "There is no way for a Mirror-Walker to leave the place of chaos once they have entered it. But if the Mirror-Walker is connected in some very strong way to another Mirror-Walker, they can call that other to rescue them. Because the mirror self comes directly to them and not through a mirror, the other can take them both back to the real world."

Ling glanced at her granddaughter who was looking at her very defiantly. "My husband thought such rescue from the place of chaos was just a myth, but David was trapped in the chaos last year and called upon Chi. Because she was asleep, somehow it was possible for her mirror self to go to him and bring him back from the chaos. When she awoke, she remembered none of it, but David told her what had happened."

Ling paused and looked down at the ground. It was obvious that she was trying not to cry. After a few moments Robert asked, "So?"

Ling answered with tears in her eyes and a voice that was almost crying. "Chi wants to go back to the van and then walk into the chaos."

When Robert and Lucy looked at her in confusion, she said, "When the Mirror-Walker goes into the mirror, they go into a bubble of mirror world that overlays the normal world. If you step outside that bubble, you are outside the mirror world, but you are not in the normal world. You are in a world of chaos where dwells the demon beasts... and fire warriors... ... and death."

She looked over at her granddaughter. There was no expression in her voice or on her face as she said, "Once she has fully left the safety of the mirror world, she cannot return. If David does not come to her, she will die in the mirror world as did her mother and her uncle."

Ling dissolved into soft tears as she apparently repeated what she said to Chi. Robert remained silent, but after a few moments, Lucy spoke up. "I can see by Chi's face that she is going to do this no matter what any of us say. Is there anything we can do to help?"

"No," Ling said between sobs. "Her mind is made up. And she must do this alone."

Chi spoke slowly to her grandmother. "She says," Ling translated, "that if she fails, then she and Beloved will die together. If she does not come back, do not make her like her uncle. End the misery of her body and keep her ashes until they can be mixed with David's."

"What do you mean?" Robert asked.

"My son," Ling replied, "died in the mirror many

years ago, but somehow his body lives on. Chou thought that, because his body did not die, Kong Wei was alive, but trapped somewhere in the chaos. I know my daughter died in the mirror. Her body lived only long enough to give birth to Chi. Should she become trapped in the chaos, Chi does not want her body to be cared for like a doll."

"Holy..." Lucy sputtered "This is beyond weird." She looked back and forth between Robert and Ling and Chi.

"What time would be best?" Ling asked softly.

"You mean," Robert answered, "what time would David most likely be asleep?"

Ling nodded her head.

He chewed on his lower lip for a moment before answering. "I'm assuming that he is still here in the US. I'm also assuming that they aren't trying to break him– just keeping him on ice. So I would say the middle of the night– three am, our time. If he's on the east coast, that's four am, if he's on the west coast that's one am. Three am would give the highest chance of David being asleep."

Ling spoke slowly to Chi. Then she stood up and said, "We are both very tired from the flight and from the change in time zones. Chi and I will attempt to get some sleep. I normally use my phone as my alarm, but we left those at David's house. Someone will have to make sure that we are awake at three for Chi to walk in the mirror."

"I've got an alarm on my watch," Robert answered. "I'll make sure you are awake."

Chapter Six
"Into the Chaos"

The alarm wasn't needed, at least not for Chi. She had slept briefly and then slipped out of the van to sit and stare at the stars. The deep valley and lack of large, nearby cities meant that thousands of stars were visible. Even the wispy trace of the Milky Way was clear in the night sky. She sat silently watching the stars and listening to the owls and frogs and katydids. Somehow she knew it was time and had just begun walking back to the van when Robert stuck his head out of his tent.

"Sergeant Garcia," he called out loudly.

"Yeah," came a muffled response from the other tent.

"Get your butt into those skinny jeans of yours and go sit in the van with Momma Ling," he barked out. "She may need some emotional support if this thing goes sideways."

"Why can't you do that?" came the sleepy response.

"Trust me," he answered back, "it would be a lot better if it were you rather than me."

A few moments later, Lucy crawled out of her tent and walked over to the van. As she stepped inside, Robert heard her say, "Oh... yeah... OK... Is this how this works?"

Momma Ling chuckled slightly and said, "You Americans are so hung up about your bodies. Yes, this is how it works... at least for a novice. Once a Mirror-Walker has gained experience and strengthened their ability to look within themselves things are different. It is always much easier unclothed in front of a large mirror, but for a master, all that is needed is enough mirror to show the opening to your soul. ... At least that is what my husband always said."

She pointed to her eye to indicate what she had meant, and then held her finger in front of her lips indicating that they should be quiet.

Meanwhile, Chi was standing nude before the black mirror, breathing deeply and concentrating on going within herself so that she could enter the mirror. The sounds of the night faded away as the blackness drew her in. Suddenly she was standing in the black van, still parked where it had been the first time she visited it.

She looked all around the van, hoping to see something which would identify it, but there was nothing unusual inside. She paused for a moment, and then stepped through the side of the van. There was nothing unusual on the outside of the van either. In fact, it was one of a dozen or so identical vans parked in a below ground car park.

The license plates on all of the vans said, "U.S. Government." Government was one of the growing list of English words which Chi knew. There were some other words on the plates, but Chi did not recognize them. Robert had already told them that they could not risk trying to look up the actual license number, so she didn't bother to memorize it.

She stood alongside the van trying to reassure herself that this was the only way to save Beloved. Finally, after several minutes, she began to walk slowly toward the ramp. She could sense, but not truly see, the boundary which she knew she had to cross. The thought crossed her mind that the bubble at the Shanghai airport had been much larger when she was there with Beloved. Maybe it was because this was underground rather than out in the open. Or maybe the bubble had been larger in Shanghai because both she and Beloved had been there. In any case, after just a few steps onto the ramp, the car park began to fade and the glow of the fires of chaos began to tinge the darkness through which she was now walking.

Almost as soon as she had fully entered the darkness, the snarling beasts began to circle her. They growled like dogs, but they were more than dogs... more even than wolves. She had no doubt that any one of them could easily tear her apart, but for some reason they did not. Instead they circled around her with their heads turned toward her so that she could see the dull red glow of their eyes.

A gap appeared in the circle as the beasts moved in closer and turned to begin walking towards her. They growled and snapped at her, but it soon became obvious that their intent was not to actually attack her, but rather to force her towards the flames which rose from a pit in the distance.

As they approached the pit, two fire warriors appeared just outside the circle of beasts. Their faces were hidden behind large, black masks which appeared to be made out of wood. Their armor was a combination of metal armor from the west, leather armor from the east, and other, unknown materials from unknown places. The swords in their hands were almost five feet long, including the long handle. The swords looked like nothing which Chi had ever seen, but most closely resembled the two-handed scimitars used in ancient China. Both warriors were rapidly flipping their swords from hand to hand so that the thick, curved, blades spun before them like propellers.

Suddenly, one of the warriors stopped his sword and held it with both hands so that it was resting with its point on the ground between his feet. He motioned to the other warrior, who stepped back several feet before assuming the same pose.

"Chi," the warrior said loudly, "you should not have come here."

The voice sounded oddly familiar to Chi. It was as

if she had heard it before. "Grandfather?" she asked in amazement.

"People always said that I sounded like my father," the warrior replied.

"Uncle Wei!" she exclaimed. "How did you get here?"

"You know how I got here," he replied. "I stepped out of the mirror bubble into the chaos. What you want to know is how I became a warrior guarding the fires of chaos."

He lifted his mask to reveal a youthful face. "Many years ago," he began, "I did what you have now done. I stupidly stepped through the mirror world boundary into the place of chaos. I thought that because of my great skills, I would become powerful in the land of chaos. But once here, I found myself with only two options."

He pointed to the fiery pit which was the only source of illumination in the darkness of chaos. "I could allow myself to be forced into the fire... Or, I could challenge and defeat one of the guardians and take his place."

He smiled at Chi. "Your grandfather was a master with staff and sword and bare hands. He taught me well and eventually the student became the master."

The smile disappeared from his face as he said flatly, "Unfortunately, I did not listen as well to the Master when he talked about life." His voice became bitter, almost angry. "Had I listened, I would never have come here. And once here, I would have chosen death in the fire over this."

His face contorted with anguish as he said, "Chi, I have no choice. As a guardian of the fire, I am joined to the darkness of chaos. I must force you into the flaming pit." Tears streamed down his face as he said, "Please do not try to fight me. You cannot defeat me! If you fight me, I will destroy you with a thousand cuts and the beasts will consume your lifeless body."

He paused as he choked back a sob, "At least the fire is quick."

"There is a third option," Chi said strongly. Then she spun, faced the beasts and cried out to the blackness above her, "Beloved, I need you. Beloved, save me!"

The darkness shimmered slightly and David stood before her. "Take my hand," he said softly.

Chi reached out and grabbed both of his hands and almost immediately they were standing in a dark room. A small amount of light filtered into the room through a window in the center of a loose-fitting door.

In the dimness Chi could just make out a wooden cot. David was asleep under a thin blanket.

"You can go home now," the mirror David said. He then shimmered slightly and was gone.

Chi stood watching David sleep for several minutes. Then she walked toward the door outlined in the darkness. As she approached, she could see that a thin piece of gray cloth covered the opening which served as a window. Upright bars created darker lines in the gray light penetrating the cloth.

For some reason the door was difficult to push through despite the fact that it wasn't all that thick. On the other side of the door was a dimly-lit, small room with a desk and several monitors sitting on tables. Four of the monitors displayed what appeared to be night vision views of a beach. The remaining two monitors, both labeled "Containment Cell," were glowing, infrared images of the dark cell. Chi smiled as she saw the reflection of the guard's face in one of the monitors.

"This is the guard room," she said softly to herself as she shimmered and disappeared.

**

Momma Ling and Lucy both startled as Chi, who had been standing rigidly staring into the mirror, suddenly started laughing and clapping her hands together. She turned to face the two women and screamed out joyfully. "Beloved is alive! He is alive! And I have found him!"

Almost dancing, Chi grabbed her grandmother's hands. "I have been where they are keeping him and I can go back. The monitor screens in the guard room are enough of a mirror... I think."

Her face suddenly changed from joy to sorrow. She stared at her grandmother for several seconds as if trying to form her words. Finally she said slowly, "Momma Ling, I have also found Uncle Wei. He has become one of the fire warriors. He is trapped in the chaos until someone defeats him."

Tears overflowed her eyes as she added, "Then he will die." She began sobbing. "He would have forced me into the fires of chaos if Beloved had not come for me," she wailed. "He did not want to, but he is controlled by the darkness."

She took several deep breaths as she tried to control her sobs. "Did he kill my mother?" she finally asked, her body shaking.

"No," Ling replied softly. "Your mother was killed by another Mirror-Walker. Your grandfather saw it happen but was too late to save her. He pursued her killer for many years."

She smiled. Her sad eyes made it a bittersweet smile. "There are no weapons in the mirror," she said softly. "When your grandfather finally caught your mother's murderer, he struck him down with his bare hands."

She took a deep breath before continuing, "Nothing can kill a Mirror-Walker while they are in the

44

mirror except the fires of chaos... or another Mirror-Walker."

"Or getting sucked out of an airplane at forty thousand feet," Chi added softly.

"What?" Ling asked in surprise.

"I did not tell you everything about what Beloved and I did together last year," She said even more softly. She looked back and forth between Lucy and her grandmother several times and then said in a more normal tone of voice, "But that is for another time. For now, we must decide how we can rescue Beloved."

The van door opened slightly and Detective Nash's voice could be heard asking, "Are you decent?" He paused a moment and said, "I was listening outside the door, but I didn't want to come in if you weren't decent."

"Just a moment," Ling said as she handed Chi the terrycloth robe. Momma Ling then slid the van door open.

The first thing Robert did when he entered the van was to turn to Chi and ask almost angrily, "When in the hell did you learn to speak English?"

Chi looked at him in confusion and then said something rapidly in Chinese to Momma Ling. Ling, also looking confused, turned to Robert and said, "She was speaking to me in Mandarin."

"I don't understand Chinese," Lucy said, "but I understood every word you both said."

Ling said something quickly to Chi who faced Robert and spoke rapidly. When Robert just looked back at her, Ling said, "She asked, 'Can you understand me now?'"

"Maybe it's like when I can sometimes see where you have been when you first come out of the mirror," Robert said. "Maybe the mirror bubble or whatever you call it spills out of the mirror for just a little while or goes into the Mirror-Walker's body or something."

He looked over at Lucy, who shrugged her shoulders and said, "Don't look at me for an explanation. My weird meter went off-scale a long time ago."

Chi joined Robert in laughter as soon as her grandmother translated what Lucy had said. Then Chi said very slowly and with much difficulty, "What now?" She followed that with a quick burst of Chinese spoken to her grandmother.

"She says," Ling explained, "that she is trying to learn English, but it is a very hard."

"Ask her," Robert said, "if she would rather use you as a translator or go into the mirror and join us out at the picnic table."

Ling spoke quickly with Chi and then said, "Picnic table."

"OK, then," Robert said. "The three of us will go sit at the picnic table and give Chi time to join us."

As they were getting out of the van, Chi yelled something to her grandmother. Ling turned around and pulled something from the van before walking over to the table.

When they got there, Ling carefully spread a blanket on the bench on one side of the table and then sat down, leaving space alongside her for Chi to join them. "She said the bench is cold and rough and asked me to put the blanket down for her to sit on," Ling explained.

"I thought she couldn't actually feel things in the mirror," Lucy said.

"She feels things differently when she is in the mirror," Ling said with a slight laugh. "It is not really hot or cold or smooth or rough. But there is no clothing in the mirror. If you knew the bench was cold and rough, even not really feeling it, would you sit on it naked?"

"Point taken," Lucy said with a big smile. "Point taken."

"So, what's the plan," Lucy then asked, looking at Robert who was sitting next to her.

"Let's give Chi a chance to get here," he replied.

"I feel like I'm at a seance," Lucy said.

"That would be easier," he said with a huff. "At least she could blow a trumpet or something."

"I think she is here now," Ling said. "What are we going to do to free David?"

"Freeing David," Robert said, "is just the first part of this... a *VERY* important part, but we have to find out who is behind all this or none of us will be safe." He looked around the table and then over at the van, "If they took David because of what they thought he could do, nothing will stop them from coming after us all."

Ling looked over at the empty blanket next to her and said, "Do not worry, Chi, the first thing we will do is rescue Beloved."

Chapter Seven
"A Visit to Beloved"

Very early the next morning, Robert, Lucy, Momma Ling, and Chi sat around the picnic table eating breakfast. The two fishing poles were leaning against a nearby tree with the tackle box at their base. It was the middle of the week, so they basically had the campground to themselves. The only other campers were some canoeists who were camped near the trees that separated the campground from the highway. Since the sun was barely peeking over the bluffs into the river valley, they were still asleep in their tents. Even so, the wary detective spoke in a low voice and turned his head often to scan the area around them.

"The way I see it," he began, "Chi has to go back to wherever it is that David is being held and see if she can see anything that will identify the place. He could be anywhere."

"Anywhere with a beach," Lucy interjected.

"Yeah," Robert agreed, "but that only narrows it down to someplace near water."

"It is early," Ling said. "If Chi can see where the sun is, it will tell us much about the beach. Also, the sea looks much different than a lake."

She then paused to speak at length with Chi.

"Tell her to look for anything unusual," Robert said. "... or highway signs if there are any... or license plates on cars."

Ling translated to Chi who looked upset. Chi turned to Robert and said slowly, "I not child." She then said several things rapidly to her grandmother in Mandarin.

Ling smiled at Chi and then said, "Chi apologizes for her disrespect, but asks you to remember that just because she does not speak your language, it does not mean she cannot think on her own."

"Tell her I meant no disrespect," Robert answered. "And she is correct. I'll be more careful with my respect for her in the future."

Before Ling could translated, he added, "But we do need to pool our ideas if we are going to figure this out."

"I will tell her all that you said," Ling replied before beginning to speak with Chi.

After a few minutes, Chi stood and walked toward the van. "She is going to go back to where Beloved is being held," Ling explained. "She says that she will explore as far as she can within the bubble."

Once the van door was closed, Robert coughed lightly and said, "Kong Ling, I mean no disrespect, but Kong Jing seems to be a very intelligent young woman. Why was she never taught English?"

Ling looked back at him for several moments with an intentionally very blank expression. Then she sighed and said, "My husband was once a part of the government... a highly placed part of the government. He used his... special skills... to avoid the multitude of pitfalls which befell many in those days. But, some began to suspect that he– and perhaps his family– had special skills. My son and my daughter were used by the government for evil purposes. Chi's mother, Kong Li, refused to do all that was asked of her. That eventually led to her death at the hands of another Mirror-Walker the government had under its control.

"My son, Kong Wei, did all that they asked of him, but became corrupted by the power he felt it gave him. That eventually led to his death... that I now find is worse than death.

"Kong Chou and I decided to hide our little Chi from those in power. He resigned from the government citing poor health. We retired to a small fishing island near Penglai where Chi could be raised as just a fish island girl. Such girls are often uneducated. We could not have that, but we felt that if she showed that she knew English it would draw too much attention to her."

Ling slumped her shoulders and stared at her hands. It looked as if she were going to break into tears, but she stiffened her back and brought a smile to her face before saying, "We should have known that one cannot escape their fate. She is a Mirror-Walker. That is how she was born... that is how she will live... and that is perhaps how she will someday die."

All three then looked over to the van. No one said anything as they waited silently for Chi to accomplish what only she could do.

**

Chi stood in front of the black mirror breathing deeply. It took extra effort to calm herself and suppress her anxiety knowing that she was going to once again see Beloved, even if he would be unable to see that she was there.

The blackness of the mirror faded away as she called her destination to mind, and soon she found herself standing in the small guard room outside David's cell. The room itself was not much brighter than it had been the night before, but a brighter light of some sort was obvious around a doorway. She would investigate that in a minute, but first she had to see Beloved.

David was standing more or less in the center of his small enclosure, staring up at the ceiling. At first she couldn't understand what he was doing, but then she realized that there was a small pipe sticking down slightly through the low ceiling of the cell. David's face was illuminated by a circle of sunlight. Evidently the pipe, for some reason, stuck up through the roof of the building they were in.

She reached up and touched his cheek. He didn't seem to notice, but his face seemed less strained as her fingers moved across his chin and lips. Chi moved close to him and said, "Soon, Beloved." She then turned and pushed back through the door of the cell.

The ceiling of the guard room was much higher than the ceiling in the cell. Three men sat in the room. One was sitting at one of the empty tables and seemed to be reading a magazine; one was seated at the desk filling out some sort of report; and the third was at the monitor table, carefully watching the bank of monitors. One of the two monitors which were labeled, "Containment Cell" showed part of David's empty bed. The other was currently focused on the back of his head. The guard reached out and moved a joystick on the table and the camera swivelled from side to side, showing the entire cell.

Chi stopped to examine the four monitors which had shown the beach at night. Now that it was day, there were people walking on the beach. It appeared that two of the cameras faced the ocean while the other two faced the other way. One of those cameras showed a long stretch of road that was nearly covered with sand. The other showed a curving road that seemed to circle around a tall tower of some sort.

Chi walked to the door which was apparently the entrance to the guard room. Unlike the door to Beloved's cell, this door was very easy to push through. Once through the door, she found herself in an almost well-lit area facing another, much larger door. This door appeared old. It had once been green, but was now badly rusted as if it were made of iron or steel. It apparently had been neglected for many years and sagged slightly on its hinges so that it didn't quite close in its frame. The door also ended several inches before the top of the opening. That may or may not have been part of the original design. In any case, a significant amount of sunlight was streaming through the openings left by the partially closed door. As Chi struggled to push herself through that iron door, she realized that the door to Beloved's cell must also be made of steel.

The outside sunlight caused Chi to squint her eyes. The sun was only a little way up into the sky and yet it was brilliant off the white sands and sparkled brightly on the breaking waves. It surprised Chi that the beautifully clear waves breaking on the beach seemed to be almost green rather than blue or brown. Perhaps the oceans appeared green here in America. She also marveled that the water was so much cleaner and clearer than the polluted muck which surrounded her small island at home.

She turned completely around scanning for anything useful. For some reason, the bubble stretched much farther out into the ocean than it did on the side with the road. Perhaps it was stretching to match her fascination with the waves. Or perhaps the side with the road was shorter because it did not appeal to Chi like the ocean did. On the road side, she could see the base of a large tower across a road from where she stood. The very top of the tower, however, vanished into the mists which marked the edge of the bubble. What she could see reminded her of pictures she had seen of coastal watch towers.

The large steel door through which she had exited seemed to be built into the side of a hill. Examining the hill further, and walking around and as far up onto its side as the bubble would allow, Chi was able to see that the hill itself was artificial and seemed to cover a concrete structure of some sort. Two large guns protected by heavy steel shields, stuck out of the edge of the hill.

While she was standing on the side of the hill, a car drove up. It had government plates and some writing on the side which Chi couldn't read. An older man, dressed in a green uniform and wearing a strange hat, got out of the car and walked up to the door. The door squealed as he forcefully opened it and stepped inside. Chi followed him back into the darkness.

"What's he doing today?" the man asked in a very gruff voice as he took off his hat and set it on one of the tables. His hair had once been a dark brown, but was now showing more than a trace of gray.

"Staring up the damned vent tube like always," one of the guards answered. "He does that for hours at a time. I think he's gone nuts."

Another of the guards laughed and said, "Maybe he thinks someone will see him and rescue him."

"Just so he stays fully clothed and doesn't look into any mirrors," the older man barked out. "The Boss is real specific on that. Clothes on! No mirrors! No shiny surfaces! Whatever it is that he does needs a mirrored surface and evidently he needs to be naked to do it."

"Yeah," the third guard said, "but him standing still like that all day gives me the creeps."

The man moved over to look at the cell monitors. "I don't care if he turns into a statue," he spat out. "Just so he can't do whatever it is that he does with mirrors until he is doing it for us."

As the man picked up his hat and turned back toward the door the first guard said, "Even if he does his mumbo jumbo, there's no way he can report back to the President or the First Lady."

"You better hope not," the man said. He set his hat on his head and turned back to glare at the three guards. Then he said coldly. "You three need to watch him like your life depends on it." As he once more turned to leave he added loudly, "... because it does!"

After the squeal and squeak indicated that the outer door had closed, the guard who had been reading the magazine said, "Asshole!"

"Yes," said the guard at the desk, "but he happens to be the asshole we work for, so do your job and check perimeter security. Make sure the tourists aren't on the roof near the vents and antennas."

The guard in front of the monitors grumbled, "We can see everything in the monitors. It's bad enough that we have to walk around once an hour. Why does one of us have to stand watch from outside every morning and every night?"

"Because the cameras can't point into the sun, peabrain," the first guard replied. "It damages them. That means there's a blind spot to the east as the sun rises and to the west as it sets. So for an hour and a half in the morning and an hour and a half at sunset, one of us has to be outside watching, just in case."

He tapped the watch on his wrist and continued, "And to make sure that something doesn't get past the cameras, one of us walks out there each hour and looks official. Remember, if any of the tourists get too nosy, just tell them the area is restricted for their safety. It's that way all over this damn fort, so they'll believe you."

The other two guards continued to grumble quietly as the one went back to his monitors and the other walked outside. Chi pushed back through the cell door so that she could look once more at Beloved before she stepped back out of the mirror.

Chapter Eight
"Not Quite a Rescue"

Robert had a fire going by the time Chi exited the van. He and Momma Ling and Lucy were sitting around it on large logs which the detective had scrounged from somewhere. As Chi joined them, she was momentarily distracted by the shrill squeal of a young woman. Evidently the canoe campers had broken camp and were setting off down river. The squeal came when one of the girls discovered the hard way that the river just downstream of the canoe launch was much deeper than expected. She also discovered that the early spring runoff in the river was very cold.

"We're alone now," Robert said, "but we still need to speak softly. Voices can carry a long way up and down the river."

Ling translated what he had said and Chi nodded her head. She then began to report what she had seen and heard. It took a long time with her stopping every few sentences and Ling translating what she had said. As Chi spoke, Robert and Lucy both had a few short questions, but for the most part, they remained quiet until she had finished.

"Translate or van?" Robert asked when she had finished her report.

Ling translated both the question and Chi's response. "She says that it is easier to listen in the mirror, but she has been in the mirror a lot in the last two days and is very tired." Ling smiled at Chi and said, "She wants to be sure she is able to go back into the mirror to rescue Beloved if we can think of a way to do that."

"OK," Robert replied. "I guess the first thing we need to do is figure out where this fort or whatever is located."

"We know it's by the ocean," Lucy said, "and the beach faces more or less south."

"It has to be on the east coast or the gulf," Robert added, "because the sun was already up when Chi went there."

"I think it is near a harbor," Ling said. "What Chi has described sounds like old wartime coastal defenses that would normally be guarding a harbor or a port."

She held up her empty hands and said, "If I had my phone, I could look this up on line to see what might match those descriptions."

"Then it's time to go back on the grid... anonymously," Robert declared.

"And how do we do that?" Lucy asked.

"We go to college," he answered with a grin. When Lucy and Ling looked very confused, he explained. "There's a college in Decorah. That's a town about 30 miles from here. Chi is the right age to be looking at colleges so we won't look that unusual on campus. There are computer terminals in the admin building that are open to the public. I've used them before when I was here on vacation."

***

An hour later, the four of them were walking across campus from a parking lot to one of the central buildings which housed the food services and admissions offices. "I could have parked in one of the visitor spots," Robert said, pointing to a lot alongside the building, "but they have pretty good security here and I didn't want anyone running a random plate check."

The computers were located more or less in the main lobby of the building in front of what appeared to be a student lounge. Evidently the cafeteria was downstairs, but a coffee shop of some sort was alongside the lounge.

They had to wait about twenty minutes for one of the terminals to come open. Robert bought coffee for everyone while they waited. No one took notice of them as they sat and talked softly, nor did anyone notice as they clustered around the terminal when Ling began typing on the keyboard.

After several minutes, Ling said in exasperation, "There are hundreds of coastal defense forts which face south. This is going to take a long time."

"There are big, blue oceans on three sides of this country," Robert said, shaking his head. "Even ruling out the Pacific, that's a lot of area to cover."

Ling translated his comment to Chi who began shaking her head and speaking rapidly. "She says," Ling replied, "not blue, green– like green glass... and the water is very, very clear."

"I know where they are," Lucy suddenly blurted out loudly. She then looked around to see if her outburst had drawn any attention to them, but the students in the lounge area didn't seem to notice.

"Pensacola, Florida," she said firmly. "The area around there is called The Emerald Coast because of the green water. There's a big fort at the entrance to the bay."

Ling typed "Pensacola Fort" into the search engine and it automatically brought up "Fort Pickens." She then switched to a search for images using "Fort Pickens."

She had scrolled down through perhaps a hundred images when Chi suddenly yelped and pointed at the screen. Her finger was on an image of a large WWII spotter or gunnery ranging tower. "She says," Ling said, "that is the tower she saw."

Ling clicked on the image of the tower which then had a link to a map program which gave a satellite view of the tower. When she zoomed out slightly from the tower itself, Chi again pointed to the screen and outlined a gun with her finger. "Battery 234, Santa Rosa Island, Florida," Ling said quietly. "That is where David is being held."

"Makes sense," Robert said softly. "Portions of those old shore defense batteries are sealed off from the public to prevent vandalism... and other things. The man in uniform was probably a park ranger, or at least was wearing a ranger's uniform."

"So how do we get David out of there?" Lucy asked.

"Let's talk about that over ice cream," was his response.

They drove through town to a place called "Whippy Dip" which served ice cream which you had to either eat in your car or at small tables placed outside in front of the serving windows. After they had seated themselves at one of the open tables, Momma Ling said softly, "You are about to propose something that Chi– and perhaps I– will not like."

"What gave me away?" Robert asked.

"You are a man," Ling replied dryly. "When a man wants a woman to do something she may not want to do, he softens her up with food or gifts."

She paused and looked intently at the detective. Then she asked, "What is it that you want Chi to agree to?"

Robert became very serious. "We need to leave David in place for now."

When Ling bristled, he quickly added, "He's safe for now, even if he isn't very comfortable. If we spring him, The Boss– whoever that is– will know we're on to them. And who knows what they'll do then?"

He looked over at Chi and said, "This is much more important than one person. We need to rescue David, but it's even more important to stop The Boss."

As Ling translated the detective's words, Chi's eyes began to fill with tears.

"I have an idea!" Lucy exclaimed loudly. When several customers turned to look at her, she said, more softly, "An idea that we need to discuss back at the campground."

***

There was no conversation in the van as they wound their way back through the country roads to the campground. Once there, they remained quiet as they gathered once again around the picnic table.

Lucy finally broke the silence. "I think Chi would be better off listening to us through the mirror," she said quietly and then waited for Ling to translate. Chi nodded her head and walked back to the van. Ling followed her and returned carrying the blanket for the bench.

"OK," Robert said after giving Chi time to get into the mirror, "what's your great idea?"

"What if we only rescue part of David?" Lucy said.

Robert opened his mouth as if to say something, but instead just let out a big breath and motioned for Lucy to continue.

"What if, for now, we only rescue the mirror David?" she asked as she looked back and forth between Ling and Robert.

"And how do you propose to do that?" he asked.

"Momma Ling," Lucy said, "what was it you said about a master and walking in the mirror?"

Ling paused a moment and then said, "For a master, all that is needed is enough mirror to show the opening to your soul."

Lucy held up her hands with her thumbs and pointer fingers formed together in a circle about two inches across. "Would a mirror this size be enough?" she asked.

"For a master," Ling answered, "yes."

"What are you thinking?" Robert asked.

"Chi said David stares all day at the vent pipe," Lucy answered. "What if we dropped a mirror down that pipe that he could stick on the ceiling of his cell. From what Chi said he should be able to reach the ceiling. As dim as it is in there, the guards probably wouldn't notice it."

"There is not enough light in his cell," Ling said. "He could not see his eye in the mirror."

"Then we hang the mirror in the pipe itself," Lucy said firmly. "The light coming around the mirror would light up his face. The mirror would have to be a little smaller, but all a master has to be able to see is his eye, right?"

"You forgot one thing," Robert said. "For a master... David isn't a master."

After a long silence, it was Ling who spoke. "You are wrong, Detective Nash," she said in her very soft, and yet very firm way of speaking English. "David Malone is more than a master. He just does not know it yet."

The sound of the van door opening caused all of them to turn suddenly toward the sound. Chi, totally naked, was running toward them. She stopped and faced Robert and said rapidly, "Beloved is my Master, my teacher, my guide. He can do this. He will do this." She then ran quickly back to the van.

"Did you hear her in English?" Ling asked.

"Yup," answered Robert.

Lucy just shook her head and said, "After this *NOTHING* will seem weird to me."

Robert was still chuckling when Chi reappeared from the van, this time wearing her terry cloth robe. She

60

spoke to her grandmother in Chinese who answered her and then said, "She asked if the language of the mirror lasted long enough for her to give you her message from her own heart. I told her it did."

"OK," Robert said. "We know what we want to do. Now all we have to do is figure out how to do it."

"What's our first step?" Lucy asked.

"Our first step is to get our asses on the road. It's at least a thousand miles to Fort Pickens and that's going to take 21 hours or more of continuous driving. I have an idea about the mirror, but we're going to have to make a stop or two somewhere along the way."

Lucy made a motion with her head indicating that she wanted him to step to the side with her. "We're all dead tired," she said softly. "It won't do us any good if we totally wear ourselves out. This is only step one of how many steps?"

Robert nodded his head and then said loudly. "OK! Listen up! We are going to stay here until morning. First light, we are heading south." He paused and then said in a more normal voice, "Everybody give all this some thought overnight. We can share any great ideas you get while we drive."

***

Robert was true to his word. The birds were still greeting the sun when he yelled for Sargent Garcia to get up. Kong Ling and Chi were already up when he knocked on the door of the van. "I made some coffee," Ling said as she opened the door. "I think we all may need it."

Robert wanted to stay off the interstates, at least while they were still in Iowa, so their route south was somewhat circuitous and limited to secondary roads. Once they got south of Iowa City, however, he pulled onto highway 218 and announced, "This is called The Avenue of the Saints because it goes from Saint Paul to Saint Louis. It's as good as an interstate in most places and will take us straight down to Saint Louis from here." He smiled and said, "But since it isn't an interstate yet, it is much less likely to have government surveillance cameras overlooking the lanes."

Around two, Lucy, who had taken over driving at the last gas stop, pulled into a fast food place for lunch. Robert suggested that they eat in the parking lot, so they all crowded together in the back of the van.

While they were eating, Robert looked at Ling and said softly, "Kong Ling, I need Chi to go back to where David is being held and to measure something for me. I'm pretty sure I know the dimensions from what she's already described, but I have to be sure."

Ling translated what he said and then translated Chi's reply, "She wants to know how she can do that? She cannot carry anything with her and she cannot move anything when she is there."

"I just need her to put her hand over the pipe," he answered. He then held up his left hand, palm down, with the fingers together. "I just need to know how big that pipe is," he continued as he held three fingers from his right hand next to the fingers of his left. "She can tell us how many fingers wide it is and we can measure her hand when she comes back."

Momma Ling explained what the detective needed and Chi nodded her head. "I'll sit up front in the driver's seat," he explained, "and you can pull the curtain. We could do it on the road, but David said it made it harder when he was bouncing around back here."

After the translation, Chi again nodded her head and Robert stepped out of the side door of the van. As he started to walk around to the driver's door, he heard Lucy say, "I'll sit up front with Robert."

When she got into the passenger seat, he grinned at her and asked, "Getting too weird for you?"

"No," she replied. Then she huffed and said, "Yes, but not for the reason you think."

When he continued to stare at her, she said, "OK, it is for the reason you think. I can handle the mirror stuff, but it weirds me out to see somebody take their clothes off in front of me."

Robert laughed. "I came from a big family," he said. "Shared a bedroom with three brothers. We ended up taking our clothes off in front of each other all the time."

"I also came from a big family," she replied, "but I was the only girl and I ended up sharing a bedroom with three brothers only when we were all really small." She glared at him. "And we did NOT take our clothes off in front of each other... ever."

***

Behind them, Chi was standing in front of the mirror. For some reason it was taking her longer than usual to go into herself. "What is wrong, my little Chi?" Momma Ling asked, speaking in Chinese.

"I am betraying him," she said sadly. "I told him I would rescue him and we are not doing that."

"If you were trapped in that room," Ling said softly, "and David came and took you into the mirror with him, would you be happy?"

"Oh, yes!" she answered back.

"If this works," Ling said, "that is what you will be doing for your Beloved."

Chi looked back at the mirror and exhaled deeply. A moment later, she was feeling the tug of the mirror as she was swept from the van to the guard's room at the bunker.

As she did last time, she first went inside the cell to brush her hands across the face of Beloved. As she did so, he smiled... and so did she. She tried to reach up and hold her hand against the pipe, but it was too high.

"I guess I'll have to go up on top the hill," she said to herself as she pushed out through the cell door and continued through the guard's room.

Once she was outside, she followed a path around the hill and then began climbing upward. A short way up the side of the hill, she could feel the darkness descending around her. She lowered herself to her hands and knees and began crawling. It felt like there was a terrible weight pressing down on her back as she crawled. She was able to crawl almost to the pipe, but about six feet short, the feeling of pressure became too great and she collapsed to the ground.

She lay there crying for a minute or two and then began dragging herself forward across the ground on her belly. She could see the rocks and thorny plants beneath her, and even though they couldn't really cut her, she cried in pain twice as she pulled herself across the final distance. Rolling over and lying next to the pipe, she reached up and put her hand over the top. Four fingers did not quite cover the opening. She added fingers from her other hand. It was very awkward, lying on the ground on her back next to the pipe, but she was able to feel the opening of the pipe and make her measurements. Five was still not quite enough, but six was too many.

She rolled back over onto her stomach and lay there breathing heavily. She could feel, but not see, the emptiness that was just beyond the barrier which had to be merely inches above her. There was one more thing she needed to do, then she would return and say goodbye to Beloved.

***

Ling stuck her head through the curtain behind the front seats. "Do you need to know the dimensions in inches or centimeters?" she asked.

"Inches," Robert answered. "Then I've got to stop at a gas station for directions and to pick up something."

"That's a first," Lucy said with a slight laugh. "You stopping to ask directions."

"I know exactly where I'm going," he replied, somewhat harshly. "I just don't know where it is yet."

Robert took over driving, which was fine with Lucy because she had no desire to go through Saint Louis near rush hour. She was a little surprised, however, when Robert took I-55 across the river into East Saint Louis and then wandered around seeming to go from bad neighborhood to worse neighborhood before finally stopping at a rather run-down gas station. There were derelict old cars stacked behind it, but the pumps looked relatively new. From the looks of the boarded-up garage doors on the front of the station, many years ago it had been a full service station, including mechanical work.

"Fill it up," he said to Lucy, "while I go inside and pay for it."

A few minutes later, when he came back and got into the driver's side of the van, he was carrying something in his right hand that looked like a rusty, mangled can of some sort or perhaps the bottom fins off of a really large firecracker.

"What is that?" Lucy said as he handed her the object.

"That," said Robert with a grin as he accelerated back out onto the road, "is a four-inch cylinder hone. You connect an extension to it and stick it in a drill. Then you spin it at high speed while you move it up and down to polish the inside of the cylinder walls when you are replacing the pistons in an engine."

When Lucy, Ling, and Chi all looked at him in total confusion, he said, "Or... you could turn it upside down and glue a mirror to the chuck. The spring that pushes the spin grinders out will hold it in the center when we lower it down the vent pipe."

He gave all of them a big smile and added, "McGyver, eat your heart out."

"How did you know you could find that here?" Lucy asked.

"Because this station is exactly like my dad's was when I was growing up," he answered. "My grandfather started the station after he came home from the war. He used to work on cars in the big bays. But those full service days are long gone. People stopped bringing in their cars, and after a while, Dad just boarded up the bays and concentrated on pumping gas and selling beer. But he never threw away any of Gramps' old tools. All I had to do was find an old, beat up place like Dad's used to be."

As he accelerated out of the station, he said, "I figured a rundown area like East Saint Louis was my best bet, but if I didn't find it here, there would be a lot of small towns between here and Pensacola."

"Why not just buy one at an auto place?" Lucy asked.

"Because the modern ones are too flimsy," he answered. "I know that makes me sound like a geezer nostalgic for the good old days when tools were rugged, but the ones Grandpa used have strong springs to push the hones out rather than just relying on weak springs and the centrifugal force from a modern, high speed drill. I needed one from the past."

"Now," said Kong Ling, "all we have to do is figure out how to get on top of that bunker and lower that down the vent pipe."

"I have an idea on that," Lucy said, "but you and Chi... and Momma Ling will have to go along with it." She paused and then added, "And we'll have to buy some swimsuits."

"Let's wait until we camp for the night to discuss that," Robert said. "There are several problems we have to overcome and it would be better if we could all give it our total attention."

Lucy started to say something, but he cut her off with, "That doesn't mean you can't think about it, just wait until we stop to discuss it."

***

Four hours later, Robert took an exit off I-24 into a national park called "Land Between the Lakes." In response to three questioning faces, he explained, "We'll camp here for the night," but then he continued down the main park road past several nice looking campgrounds. Just past the Visitor's Center, he turned off onto a narrow, two lane road that wound back into the countryside to a large campground nestled in a small valley in the rolling hills.

There was no one at the entry gate, so Robert got out and filled in a registration card. "I figured the ranger would have gone home by now," he said. "That way they don't bug us for more information to enter into the computer system."

When he got back into the van, Lucy wrinkled her nose and asked, "What is this place?"

"It's called 'Wrangler Camp,'" he answered. "It's for horses... well, for horse people. You don't have to have horses to stay here, but that's their primary campers."

"Why here?" Lucy said, her face still crinkled from the smell of hay and horses.

"Because I knew the ranger would already be gone for the day," Robert replied, "and because it's in a valley where cellphones don't work worth a crap. But mostly because I know that horse people respect privacy. They will be as friendly as all get out if you show that you are open, but if it looks like you want to keep to yourself, they will leave you totally alone."

He laughed. "And besides," he said with a smile, "would you look for us here?"

Her look, and the slight laughter from Chi when Ling translated his remark caused him to smile even more broadly.

He had picked a spot near one of the combination bathrooms and shower houses. "Why don't you all clean up or whatever," he said, "and I'll fix supper."

As he started getting out pans, Chi said something to her grandmother. Robert looked over at Ling, and she translated. "Chi said she did not know that American men were willing to cook for women."

"Tell her not to believe everything she sees on television," he replied with a smile.

**

After supper, Lucy volunteered to wash up the dishes while Robert went over to the showers. When he returned, they all sat outside at one of the picnic tables and talked. Lucy explained her plan for sneaking up onto the top of the bunker. Ling frowned, but Chi giggled when her grandmother explained the plan to her.

"It's just crazy enough to work," was all that Robert had to say about it. Then he added, "But that leaves a couple of big problems. One, I have to figure out how long the pipe is so I can make the fishing line the right length. The mirror has to be just above the end of the pipe when David looks up at it. And two, we have to somehow let David know what we're up to."

When Ling translated to Chi, she suddenly smiled and held up her right arm, bent, with her left hand held just below the wrist. "She says," Ling translated, "that this much of the pipe sticks up out of the ground."

Chi again spoke rapidly, then stood up and bent over. She held her right arm down from her body with the left hand held at about the second knuckle of her right hand. "The top of Beloved's prison is this far below ground," Ling translated. Chi clenched her right fist and moved her left hand to above her elbow, "This much of the ground is very, very hard," she added and then Chi sat down holding her hands about eight inches apart. "And that much pipe is sticking down in Beloved's prison."

"Tell her we're very proud of her," Robert said as he scribbled on a note pad. "I should've known to tell her about this before she went to measure."

"She knows that she has done well," Ling said and then translated Robert's comment.

Chi said something back and looked at Robert with a slight smile. "And she also knew," Ling translated, "that you would need to know how long the pipe was as well as how big."

"So," Robert said, "we are left with the problem of how to let David know what's happening."

Lucy spoke up. "Momma Ling, would you please ask Kong Jing if there is anywhere in the cell that the guards can't see."

Ling repeated the question and then translated Chi's answer. "She says that there is a small area in the corner with..." She looked at a loss for words. "... one of those plastic chamber pots like is beneath the bed in the camper."

"Porta-potty," said Robert.

Ling nodded and continued, "It is behind a small

wall. But the cameras can see everywhere else."

"Great!" Lucy huffed, "All we have to do is write a message on toilet paper and sneak it into the cell."

"That's it!" shouted Robert and all three women looked at him in amazement.

"We write something on a ribbon of toilet paper and drop it down the pipe," he continued excitedly. "David can put the message in the toilet and it will dissolve with the rest of the toilet paper."

"But what do we say?" Lucy asked.

Ling translated to Chi and she responded with something and then crossed her arms in front of her chest.

"OK," Lucy said, "that looks definite. What did she say?"

Ling smiled and said softly, "For a master, all that is needed is enough mirror to show the opening to your soul." She looked over at Chi and added, "She also said 'If he knows it is from me he will know that he is a master, for I am his student.'"

Robert and Lucy spent the next two hours in the van trying to write that message on a narrow strip of toilet paper. "I know that RV toilet paper is supposed to dissolve easy," Lucy said with great exasperation, "but shouldn't it at least wait until it goes down the toilet?"

Everyone laughed, but Momma Ling paused as if thinking and said softly, "I wonder..." She then looked up at the cabinets and said, "Hand me one of those paper towels."

Robert looked confused, but handed her one. She set it on top of a strip of toilet paper and asked for one of the small markers that had proved so disastrous earlier. She carefully printed out the message and then added a Chinese character at the end. "That is Chi," she said as she set down the pen. "She tells me that David can recognize that symbol. He will know that it is from her."

She lifted the paper towel. As expected, the ink had bled slightly through the towel. And on the strip of toilet paper, somewhat faint, but very legible, was the message.

"We're ready," Robert said. "It's a day's drive to Pensacola. Day after tomorrow, just before sunset, we find out if this is going to work."

Lucy said, "I think we need to make a couple of backup copies of that message just in case one gets accidentally dissolved."

Ling said nothing, but laid another strip of toilet paper on the table and pointed at the paper towels.

***

Robert and Lucy decided to break up the drive into two days. That way they wouldn't have to camp too close to Pensacola and they would be rested when they finally put the plan into action. Overnight, they pulled into a WalMart and parked between a semi and a large, bus-like camper.

Both Kong Ling and Chi were surprised at the idea that you could just park and camp in a store parking lot overnight. "Not all of them allow it," Robert explained. "But most people who park overnight go into the store to buy things... like say, swimsuits, so the store makes money out of it." He smiled and said, "Besides, the bathrooms are clean and there is usually someplace nearby to eat."

There was a fast food place inside where they ate supper. Afterwards, Robert went back to the van while the women shopped for swimsuits. All four slept in the van that night. Ling and Chi were in the bed; Lucy was in a sleeping bag on the floor; and Robert was in the passenger seat with the back pushed down as far as possible. In the morning, after he removed the cover from the windshield, he walked across the highway to a Burger King and brought back breakfast for everyone. Lucy had also bought donuts and cinnamon rolls when she went into the store to use the restroom. They all sat at the small table in the back of the van to eat breakfast and plan the day.

"A lot of things can go wrong," Robert said as he munched on a cinnamon roll. "I'll be in the van or somewhere nearby. If I hear women screaming, I will assume it's you and come in with guns blazing. We'll probably be able to rescue David that way, but everything else will be shot to hell."

Momma Ling looked at him sternly, "I assume much of what you said are what you call American idioms. I am not sure Chi would understand– or would become too afraid– if I translated directly."

She did not translate Robert's response of "I wish to God they were just idioms."

***

They timed their driving so that they went through the front gate of Channel Islands National Park about two hours before sunset. They stopped at one of the beach pullouts and Lucy, Ling, and Chi actually got out and walked along the beach for a short while before joining Robert at one of the tables on the shade porch of the shower house. They sat where they could watch the waves as they waited. As they sat, they made several last minute refinements to their plan.

Forty-five minutes before sunset, Robert said, "It's time."

It took only a few minutes to get to the bunker. Robert had decided that he needed to be closer in case something went wrong with their plan, so he busied himself examining one of the coastal defense guns at the

72

base of the bunker while the three women walked out onto the beach itself. Chi and Lucy had changed into bikinis back at the shower house. Ling, who had also changed, was wearing a much more conservative suit with a long coverup that reached almost to her knees. The two girls put a blanket down on the sand and lay down to watch the sunset. Ling walked further up the beach.

As expected, one of the guards was out on the beach side of the bunker keeping watch. The camera which normally captured the beach west of the bunker was pointed directly out to sea. Ling glanced nervously over her shoulder at the guard. Then she heard Chi giggle loudly. The guard turned toward the sound as Lucy also giggled.

He then stood transfixed as he watched Lucy and Chi pull each other close and wrap their arms around each other's bodies. Behind him, Ling slowly climbed the overgrown hill which covered the bunker. On the top were several antennas, four cameras, and an old piece of pipe sticking up out of the ground. She carefully pulled the slip of toilet paper from the pocket of her bulky beach wrap. There was a small stone glued to one end of the strip.

She dropped the paper down the tube and then pulled the cylinder hone from her other pocket. Robert had glued a small mirror to the shaft of the hone and then wrapped fishing line around the three hones themselves to compress them. He had also attached two carefully-measured strands of fishing line to the shaft. She set the hone partially into the pipe and removed the line holding it closed. When she unwrapped the last loop of line, the rusty polishing blades moved out until they just touched the pipe. She very carefully lowered it down the pipe, her breath catching the couple times when it seemed to snag momentarily on its way down.

There were two sticks tied to the top end of the fish line. She carefully placed them in an X shape on the top of the pipe and then turned and walked quietly back down the hill.

When she returned to the beach, she ran toward Chi and Lucy yelling in Chinese. When Robert heard her yell, he smiled. Chinese meant they were finished. English meant trouble.

The guard, who had been staring transfixed at the two girls on the blanket, startled and then started laughing as Ling pretended to berate the two girls in Chinese. She then pointed dramatically at the parking lot and strode angrily behind them as they marched back to the van. The sun was now almost down and the camera was turned back west. The guard was still chuckling to himself as he slipped back into the guard room.

***

When the sky turned from blue to dark gray, David sat back on his bed. That small circle of blue was all that kept him from sliding into a severe depression. He didn't even like cloudy days, and survived Iowa winters only by regularly visiting a tanning salon. Day after day in this dim prison would have destroyed him without that little circle of blue and the light shining on his face.

As he sat on his bed, something caught his eye. It looked like a large moth fluttering to the ground beneath the vent pipe. If it was a moth, he would lift it back up to the vent pipe so it could find its way back out. If it were a bird, he would have to call the guards. They really didn't understand his concern for such little things, but they would humor him by carrying the bird to the heavy main door and releasing it.

Whatever it was on the ground, however, didn't look like a bug or a bird. It was too long... and it looked like there was writing on it. He picked it up in his hands and then held them up to the pipe as if he were lifting a moth to freedom. After giving the moth time to ascend back up the pipe, he concealed the strip of paper in his hands and took it back over to his bunk. He knew that if he sat on the top of his bed with his back against the wall the guards couldn't see the upper portion of his body.

He sat carefully straightening the message and strained to read the faint writing in the dim light. His tears began to drop into his cupped hands, slowly dissolving the message. As he held the now soggy message, he said very softly, "She knows where I am." More tears flowed as he murmured, "She thinks I am a master of the mirror."

He had seen something in the vent pipe when he pretended to release the "moth," but it would draw attention to it if he went back over now to investigate. He would have to wait until morning to find out what Chi had brought him.

Chapter Nine
"A Mirror of Freedom"

Chi had insisted that she had to go into the mirror as soon as she had gotten back to the van. She was standing next to her Beloved as he lifted the paper up to the vent pipe. She was stroking his face as he cried into the message. And she was back, standing next to him, when he awoke in the morning.

As soon as he opened his eyes, David wanted to run over to the pipe to see what was there. But he knew that any difference in his routine would be suspicious to the guards. He forced himself to sit at the small table and slowly eat his breakfast. He was beginning to tire of cinnamon rolls for breakfast and sandwiches for all other meals, but he was allowed no silverware and all liquids were encased in bottles that had been wrapped with some sort of tape. He had once tried spilling some of his water out of the bottle onto the table, but his guards rushed in immediately and wiped up the liquid with some paper towels. His captors were obviously making very sure that there were no mirrors or mirror-like surfaces anywhere around him at any time. When he had finished, he set the tray at the bottom of the door and knocked twice.

"Stand clear!" ordered the guard, and David stepped back three steps.

The bottom of the door opened noisily and a hand reached in and grabbed the tray.

David smiled and turned to stand beneath the vent pipe.

"He's at it again," one of the guards said as they watched him on the monitor. "Sometimes, I wish he'd do something else just to make it interesting," he added with a laugh. "Once the sun is up, the only time he's away from that pipe is to do exercises a couple times a day. It gets pretty boring watching him do nothing."

"Interesting is not good," the other guard said gravely. "Let's keep it boring."

The guard went back to staring at David motionless in the screen. What he couldn't see was the smile on David's face as he looked up into the vent pipe. There was a small, circular mirror suspended about two inches up in the pipe. It looked like it had been pried from a woman's makeup case, which it had been. Enough light got past the mirror to illuminate his face in the mirror.

"For a master, all that is needed is enough mirror to show the opening to your soul," he said softly as he slowly shifted position so that the mirror was reflecting his left eye back into itself.

He repeated that statement twice more before he began saying softly, over and over again, "Chi. Chi. Chi. Chi. Chi."

He might not have been able to do it back at his home, but here in this cell there was nothing else to tempt his mind. When the tugging finally came, it was as if he were being drawn upward into the vent pipe, and then he was back standing in his cell looking at himself. Chi was standing next to him smiling and clapping her hands. When he turned to her, she jumped at him and grabbed him around the neck.

"We have come to free you," she said joyfully. Then she suddenly became very serious and added, "... in the mirror." She looked down at the floor and said softly, "Right now, we can only free the mirror you, but soon we will free your body also."

"How did you find me?" he asked.

"I have been here before," she said flatly, "so I was able to come to the guard room."

David looked confused. "How were you here before?" he asked. "There're no mirrors. Who brought you here?"

"You did," she answered, again looking down at the floor.

"I did!?" he yelped. "How could I bring you here? When did I do that?"

"You were asleep," she said, still looking at the floor.

David looked at her in shock as the realization of what she had to have done sank in. "You could have been trapped there forever," he said slowly. "You shouldn't have risked it."

"I knew we were connected," she said softly. "If we were not, I would not have been able to rescue you when you were trapped in the place of chaos. I knew you would come for me."

He looked at her and said, "And I knew that you would come for me."

David took a very deep breath and let it out slowly. Then he said, "What now?"

"I will return to the house on wheels," she said. "I am using the black mirror in your house on wheels. Join me there and we will talk." She shimmered and disappeared. David waited a few moments and then said softly, "Van."

When he arrived at the van, the non-mirror Chi was standing in front of the black mirror mounted on the side wall. An older Chinese woman was sitting watching her. She looked at her watch and then looked up at the mirror. "Chi said that the mirror bubble extends well beyond the picnic table. She is waiting for you there."

David pushed his way through the side door of the van. It was sitting in a small campground. Chi was standing next to a picnic table. Detective Robert Nash was sitting on one side of the table. A young Hispanic woman whom David did not know was sitting across from him.

Chi whooped in glee when David appeared and ran toward him. She hugged him and then ran back into the van. A moment later Momma Ling stuck her head out of the van and said, "He's here." A few moments after that, Chi came running back to the picnic table and stood next to Beloved.

"A few introductions first, David," Robert began. "This is Sargent Luciana Garcia. You may have met her before. She works with me and got sucked into this back in Plain City. The woman in the van is Kong Ling. She is Chi's grandmother." He laughed slightly and said, "Chi's name, by the way, is actually Kong Jing, but the mirror gave you her baby name that only her family would call her."

He waved his hand in the air and continued, "Anyway, Chi was able to signal me that something was wrong by popping in at me in my mirror while I was trying to shave. We brought her and her grandmother over here to help us find you, but whoever grabbed you tried to kill them at the airport and we had to go into hiding."

He pointed at Lucy and she said, "Right now, we are trying to track down whoever it is behind all this, but they might be high up in the government so we can't trust anyone and are working more or less on our own."

"In other words," Robert said as he tilted a bottle of beer to his lips, "just like old times."

Chi turned to him and said, "Warrior Robert wants to know if there is anything you can add that might help us find these people."

David stood a moment trying to understand all that he had just been told. "I don't know," he said to Chi, "the only people I see are the guards and the man dressed as a ranger." He stopped as if remembering something and then added, "Right after I was taken to that underground prison, a man in a suit came to look at me. They brought me out into the guard room and he just stood there staring at me for a long time. Finally, he said, 'Keep him away from anything shiny,' and walked out."

He walked back and forth in front of the table and then said, "He was just an average-looking guy in a suit... maybe a few inches shorter than I am. It was a dark suit with a regular tie and a– wait a minute!– his lapel pin. It was bigger than normal and had a strange emblem on it. The ranger who comes in every so often wears a smaller version of the same pin."

He took Chi's hand in his own and drew on the palm of her hand. "It is shaped like this. The emblem on it looks like a sword broken in two by the beak of a bird. I've never seen it before."

"Wait here," Chi said and ran back to the van. A moment later Momma Ling walked out to the table and relayed what David had told Chi.

After Ling finished speaking, Lucy shook her head and said, "Boy, and I thought working through a translator was difficult." She looked up at where David had been standing and asked, "Have you ever seen anything like it before? What were the main colors on the pin? What was the overall shape? Did you see any words or letters?"

David was actually standing behind Robert, but he heard what Lucy asked. So did Chi who had come back out and was standing next to him. "The sword was silver," he said. "The beak was sort of gray with a bit of white like a bird's head. They were both on a dark blue shield. There were some letters on the top, but they were almost too small to read. They might have been AIS or PLS or maybe PTS. I think middle letter was strangely shaped, but I'm really not sure."

Chi ran back into the van and Ling quickly walked back to the group at the table to repeat David's message.

To David's surprise, the non-mirror Chi joined them at the table shortly thereafter. She was wearing a terry cloth robe which she had tied firmly around her. She stood across the table from Robert and said very carefully– in English– "Now what?"

She then ran back into the van and, after less than a minute, reappeared next to David. They both looked down at Detective Nash as he sat thinking. "I think," he said, "that it's time to enlist my brother and some of the resources that he might be able to trust."

He looked up at where David had first been standing and said, "David, I'm really sorry that we have to leave you at the bunker for now, but we can't tip our hand yet. Hopefully they won't find the mirror and you can join us regularly."

He smiled broadly and said, "And more importantly, you can join Chi."

He gestured at the nearby river and said, "We are currently in an access area– a fishing camp– in Alabama. We're going to head to DC from here. Chi can let us know if you are with us or whatever, but she can't be in the mirror all of the time, so figure on her checking with you each morning and evening. She'll act as your messenger if there is something you need us to know."

He smiled and looked around. "I don't know how well Chi can handle the mirror with bouncing around in the van, so we're going to wait an hour to leave. You two can walk around here or just sit and talk."

He gestured toward a nearby picnic table. There was a blanket spread on the seat. "But remember," he said with mock sternness, "Momma Ling is watching you... or at least Chi, and we have to leave in an hour, sharp."

David and Chi looked at each other. Chi giggled and David could not help smiling broadly. They walked over to the picnic table and sat on the blanket.

"Momma Ling must have put the blanket out earlier," Lucy said.

"Actually," Robert said, "I put it there when I came out to build the fire this morning. I may be thick, but I do catch on eventually."

"I'll keep that as our little secret," she replied.

***

An hour later they were on the road. Nine hours after that they were pulling in to a WalMart parking lot in Roanoke, Virginia. Robert decided that a celebration was in order and they actually ate supper that night in a restaurant near the WalMart. The next day was four more hours of driving to get to Prince William Forest Park in Dumfries, Virginia.

The park is part of the United States National Park System and, as its name implies, is over 15,000 acres of natural forest. A small entry fee gets you a pass for your vehicle that is good for a week. There was no guard on duty at the front gate, so Robert had to stop at the Visitor's Center to pick up a pass before driving to the Oak Ridge Campground inside the park.

As they wound back through the trees on the narrow road to the campground, Robert said, "This time of year they should have an opening. This is a pretty popular spot for tent campers and vans once school's out and the weather warms up a little more... especially on weekends. If I'm wrong we will stay another night in a parking lot somewhere and then find someplace else tomorrow."

When Lucy looked over at him, he continued, "There is a regular RV park around the side by the highway where most people with bigger units stay. These campgrounds in the park itself are pretty primitive, but they will allow small RVs and vans like this one to camp there."

Gesturing at the dense woods which surrounded them, he added, "This is about as far off the grid as I can get and still be close to the White House."

The campground was only about half full so Robert parked the van in one of the more secluded spots and walked back up to the front to sign them in. This close to DC he was afraid that someone might ask for a driver's license, so he registered as Marvin Wentworth from Dubuque. It was a false ID which Robert sometimes used in the field. It wasn't fully backstopped, but the license would show good if run through the system to verify ID and that was all he really needed at this point. He had stopped on the way in to empty the sanitary stuff and fill the van's water tank so they were all set.

"I stayed here in a tent a couple years ago," he said as he started putting the outer cover on the front windshield. "It's pretty quiet most of the time and the restrooms are adequate. It's only about forty miles from Washington. And..." He pointed slightly south. "... right next door to Quantico Marine Base."

"Can we trust the Marines?" Lucy asked.

"You can trust a jarhead to follow orders," he said. "The question is, can we trust the person giving the orders?"

He then said, "There's nothing we can do until tomorrow. Why don't the three of you take time to clean up or whatever? I've got something I have to work on."

Lucy looked at Ling and said, "I think we've been told to take a hike."

When Ling looked slightly confused, she quickly added, "Another American idiom. Robert wants us to leave him alone for a while."

"Oh," Ling said. "But a good idea nevertheless. These are beautiful woods and there are very nice trails."

As the three started to leave, Robert called out to them, "Be careful!"

Lucy turned and smiled as she called back, "Always am."

Robert noticed that she was back to wearing her tight jeans and the bulky sweatshirt. She also had her hand deep in the sweatshirt pocket.

After they were gone, he sat at the picnic table drawing and redrawing what looked like crossword puzzles on a piece of paper. Something was not going right. He was cursing softly under his breath as he kept repeatedly starting over. After crumpling up what had to have been his tenth attempt he said aloud, "Damn, I hope he remembers how to do this better than I did."

Finally, after several more tries, he seemed satisfied with his latest attempt. He spent several minutes copying the letters back out of the square and smiled broadly. Then he went to the van and got out one of the burner phones. After putting the battery in place, he sent a series of ten short texts. As soon as the last text was sent, he removed the battery and put the phone back in the duffle.

All ten texts were to his brother Mark's personal cellphone. The first text had been a series of numbers and letters which read:

01

120902OLPRDYTABABHTN

The next nine texts were almost identical. All were exactly twenty-three characters. The number at the beginning was to guarantee the message would be reassembled in proper order if the texts were not delivered in the order in which they were sent.

It would take a computerized code breaker hours or even days to break the cipher, but it was a marvelously simple one dating back to the Civil War. It wasn't used in modern times primarily because the entire message had to be received in order to decode it. Robert and Mark has used this code to send short messages back and forth to each other when they were young boys growing up.

Basically, it was a variation of "magic squares." The first two numbers said the square should be twelve by twelve, so the message would contain 144 characters. Anything beyond that was not part of the message and sent only to confuse people. The next two numbers said to begin decoding after nine false characters. There was no need to say how many false characters followed the message. In this case anything after the 153rd character was false. The last two numbers indicated that the message itself used every second letter. During Civil War times, that information was sent separately or known only to the messenger carrying the coded message.

All you needed to do was arrange the message in the proper-sized square and then read up diagonally from the proper starting point - usually the upper left corner. When you reached the edge of the square, you looped from top to bottom or to the other side and kept going. If you ran into your previous characters, you dropped down one square and continued. For a twelve by twelve square, the maximum message would be 144 characters. In some ways, it was the Civil War version of an encrypted Twitter message.

The women had returned from their walk by the time he was finished. Lucy joined him at the fire as he was burning the papers on which he had created the message. "If I did this right," he said flatly, "and if my thumbs hit all the right keys while I was texting, Mark will pick me up tomorrow at noon in front of the Jefferson Memorial."

"Where do you want us to wait?" Lucy asked.

"Right here," he answered. "Just take me up to the Springfield Metro station first thing in the morning and I'll ride in with the commuters. I'll blend in with the tourists and take the tram that goes to all the tourist spots while I kill time. If I'm not back in forty-eight hours, drive to the entrance of the White House and say you have an appointment with the First Lady that was arranged by Agent Mark Nash. He will come to the gate and you can tell him what's going down. That will at least put you under Secret Service protection."

"What about you?" she asked.

"If I'm not back here by tomorrow night," he answered very softly, "then assume that I'm dead and that this goes a hell of a lot higher that we thought."

"I think I'll wait to tell Chi and Momma Ling that last part until I have to," Lucy said glumly.

"I know it's dangerous contacting my brother like this," Robert said. "They've probably got somebody watching the White House, but we need to know what that lapel pin means. I hope I can describe it well enough so they can trace it down."

"You won't have to," said a soft voice from behind them.

Both Lucy and Robert startled as Kong Ling stepped around in front of them. "And you will not have to tell me– or not tell me– what it means if you are not back by tomorrow night."

She sighed and said, "I have been through government intrigues before. I know the risks... and how to hopefully avoid them."

She then held up a piece of paper with a drawing on it. The drawing had been done with the markers from the van. "Chi drew this while David was still here." Her voice softened greatly as she said, "She has been in the mirror much too much these past few days and it has exhausted her. She is asleep in the van."

Laying the paper on the table she said, "David said that this is very close to what the lapel pins looked like." Pointing to the top of the shield, she said, "While Chi was drawing this, David realized that the reason the middle letter looked strange was that it was actually also a sword. He is pretty sure that it is says 'PTS', if you take the sword to be a 'T'."

She looked up at Robert and said flatly, "And I think I know who they are."

Lucy and Robert stared at her with wide open eyes. "There are some within my country," she began, "who look back at the years of what you call 'The Cold War,' and see them as a time of peace, like the peace the Western world saw under the Roman Empire. They believe that if a similar state of Cold War existed between the United States and China, then the other, smaller powers of the world would be forced to join one side or the other as they did during the Cold War and there would be a return to Pax Romana, the Peace of Rome."

She took a deep breath and continued, "If you translate the name of that movement into English, it becomes 'Peace Through Strength.'"

Putting her finger on the T of PTS, she said, "They use a broken sword as their symbol. I think their American counterparts do also."

"Are you telling me," Robert sputtered, "that a bunch of high-ranking leaders in this country... and in yours... want to take the world to the brink of war in hopes of having peace?"

"The Cold War years," Ling said slowly, "were times of prosperity and growth for both the United States and China. There are many who look back nostalgically at those days and would want to return to them. And there are many in Russia who would like to see them return to the world stage as a leading power."

"That's crazy," he muttered loudly.

"But it makes sense," Lucy said. "Everyone wants to be powerful and everyone wants peace. It would be pretty easy to lure young idealists with the idea of peace and a lot of military and government people with the idea of power."

"Our government," Ling said sadly, "has been ignoring these people for years as harmless fringe lunatics. Apparently so has yours."

"They may be lunatics," Robert said angrily. "But they are no longer harmless. Nor are they fringe. No matter how crazy they are, they're now buried deep within our government."

"Well," Lucy said slowly, "there's nothing else we can do right now. What do we do with the rest of our day?"

"I would say," Robert answered, "that we sit around camp and enjoy the peace and quiet. We may not get another chance to relax once things start moving."

Chapter Ten
"A Trip to the White House"

Mark Nash always carried two cell phones. When he was on duty, his personal cell phone was always shut off. When he was off duty... well, a Secret Service agent assigned to the First Lady of the United States was never really off duty. The first family, however, was eating with some diplomats and others and were inside the White House under the full protective net of the Secret Service. Most of her regular security detail was eating in a staff dining room near the kitchen. It was one of those times when Mark felt safe turning on his personal cell and checking for messages.

He was surprised that he had thirteen messages. Three of them were normal texts from friends. The other ten were in a code that looked like something from his childhood. He looked around as he scanned the texts. They were out of order, but Robert evidently knew they might be and had keyed them with a prefix number. "I need to check something at my desk," he said to the agent next to him and walked out of the dining room.

His office was actually a duty station just outside the Presidential living quarters. He sat at the small desk and wrote out the texts in the correct order on a sheet of paper. Then, ignoring the initial numbers and the first nine false characters, he counted twelve characters and drew a line, then another line, then another and another and another.

He once again wrote out the message, this time in twelve rows of twelve characters. It read:

```
A B H T N Y S O A I O D
E F R X E T I J J X X I
D O E B X K R 5 S F F Y
O W T 3 P D P Z N W I I
K L 4 U T X R 3 A D F J
T 5 X Q O O O I V 3 C Q
```

```
3 U P T E F S W D B A 5
E S T W O S A S I U 2 S
U X F B L F L K B D F D
S 3 N K D Z P T Y X K L
F 5 L L E Q S Y A D M W
N Z X K T O R D C W E J
```

He marked the A in the upper right corner and began transcribing the message. When he was done it read, "ALL SAFE X DAVID HELD FORT PICKENS BATTERY 234 X SAFE X PICKUP TRAM STOP JEFFERSON NOON X"

He smiled slightly at the memory of the many times that he and Robert had used this code to send simple messages that could not be deciphered by their parents. Then his face hardened. This was no longer a game and lives depended on this message. They were safe. That was good. Robert's repeating that David was safe probably meant that a rescue should not yet be attempted. He would have to speak to the First Lady and the President tonight after their other responsibilities had been completed.

***

As the President and First Lady stood sharing goodbyes with the various diplomats and dignitaries who had been present for the dinner, Mark Nash stood at his post several feet behind the First Lady. After everyone had made their exit and the First Couple turned to move toward their living quarters, Mark stepped forward and coughed softly.

"I have a message from our missing investigators," he said softly, handing Helena a folded slip of paper. She glanced down at it and handed it to her husband. The President took a moment to read it and then said, "We'll talk upstairs in the hallway." He and the First Lady then continued their short journey home to the living quarters.

Once they were away from all windows and anyone who might overhear them, the President said, "What does this mean?"

"It means David is alive," Mark said. "And it means that my brother thinks he needs help with something."

"Do we need to send the Marines in for a rescue?" the President asked.

"He was specific that David is safe." Mark answered. "I think that means that we should wait. He also said they are all safe, so this is about something else."

"What do you think it is?" Helena asked.

"I have no way of knowing," Mark answered, "that's why I'm picking him up tomorrow at noon at the Jefferson Memorial."

"Do we need a protection detail?" the President asked.

"I think his greatest protection at this point," Mark replied, "is blending in with all the tourists. If I know him, he's probably wearing a loud shirt with a big camera hung around his neck."

"Be careful," the President said, "and keep us in the loop."

"Will do, sir," Mark replied. He then nodded at the First Lady and walked back to the duty station to hand over protection to his night replacement.

***

The only thing which Mark had gotten wrong in his description of what his brother would look like was the floppy hat which Robert wore to make it harder to see his face. He was standing near the tram stop with his camera up to his face. That guaranteed that no one could see his face, and more importantly, that the automatic facial recognition software in the street surveillance cameras couldn't get a hard lock. He only took the camera away from his face while he was turning or looking down. Then he would again raise it as if trying for that perfect tourist photo and watch for his brother through the camera's monitor.

Mark pulled up in a standard-issue black, government SUV and Robert immediately got in. His first words were, "I need to talk to the President, immediately."

"Jeez, Robert," his brother exclaimed. "That's not as easy as it sounds. Beyond getting you into the White House, there are schedules and appointments and God knows what else. It would have to be really important for you to just come bursting in."

Robert pulled the drawing of the Peace Through Strength pin from his pocket and said, "This organization wants to start a Cold War with China and take us back to Mutually-Assured Destruction. And two of the Senators at last night's shindig were wearing that lapel pin just below their American flags."

Mark looked over at him for several seconds and then reached into his coat pocket. He pulled out his official phone and said, "Contact Priority One." A moment later he said curtly, "This is Nash. I need to speak to the First Lady."

He continued speaking as they wound their way through DC traffic to the lower entrance of the White House. Mark showed his ID to the guard at the gate, who said curtly, "I will need some authorization for your passenger."

"Will my word do?" a pleasant voice said from behind him.

The guard turned toward the voice and then snapped to attention, "Yes, Ma'am, it would," he replied.

"Do not log the passenger in," the First Lady said firmly.

"But I have to log all visitors," the guard replied.

"Don't make Douglas walk out here," Helena said through her teeth while still holding her smile. "He wouldn't like that. ... And neither would you."

"Yes, Ma'am," the guard answered as he shifted the switch to bring the portal protection into the open state.

"I will meet you inside," the First Lady said as she and her protection detail turned and walked back toward the house. Mark continued on toward the underground parking under the lawn of the White House.

A few minutes later, Robert said to his brother, "Wow! I've never been in the Oval Office before."

"You were here at the White House last year," Mark said.

"Yeah," he replied, "but I never got to come in here."

"Well, quit acting like a yokel," Mark snapped. "You'll embarrass me."

"I think this yokel was quite instrumental in saving my wife last year," a deep voice said from the doorway.

"Yes, Mister President," Mark replied as he straightened almost to attention.

Douglas Travis turned to Robert and said, "What is so important that you had to see me immediately?"

Robert unfolded the drawing and started to lay it on the desk. He stopped with the paper several inches above the desk and said, "May I?"

"Go ahead," the President said as he walked around behind the desk. "I assume that is what you came to show me."

"The people who kidnaped David," Robert explained, "wear this lapel pin. Kong Ling thinks it is

93

the 'Peace Through Strength' organization. There is a similar group in China. They think that if the world returns to a Cold War we will return to a Package Romanoff... or something like that."

"I think my brother means Pax Romana," Mark said, "but I understand what he means."

The President's voice hardened as he said, "And I understand the appeal. Our world is torn apart by a thousand little wars with small bands of terrorists operating all over. Back in the good old days of MAD it was just two superpowers trying to kill each other off. People felt safer even though they could be incinerated in a nuclear war at any moment."

"Two of the senators at your party last night," Robert said quickly, "were wearing that pin. And they were talking about how they could guide you wherever they wanted just by rattling your cage with a couple of negative tweets."

The President flared red, but calmed himself. "I'm working on that," he said quietly. "But how do *YOU* know what they were saying?"

"Chi crashed your party," Robert said with a grin. "She checked everybody out and listened in on anyone that looked interesting." He shrugged. "I told her not to, but she is probably here with us right now... David is probably here, too."

"Oh, my God," the President said. "Is there *ANY* defense against them?"

"Mutually assured Mirror-Walkers," Robert said with a grin. "You've got an American boy and a Chinese girl who are both very loyal to their own countries and very insistent that their special abilities not be used as weapons of war or espionage."

He smiled at the President and said, "I'm supposed to deliver a message from Chi. If you pressure David into working for you, she will work against you. Kong

Ling said she will see that the same message– in reverse– gets to the government of China."

"But for now?" asked Helena, who was standing next to her husband.

"For now," Robert replied, "they are willing to work for peace... true peace."

The President sat down behind his desk. He was obviously thinking rapidly. He looked up at Mark and Robert and said, "Do you know the difference between a group of crack-pots and a terrorist cell?"

He paused as everyone, including his wife, looked at him in total confusion.

With a smile, he answered his own question with "Funding."

He picked up the drawing once again and said, "What you said about the two senators got me thinking, These Peace Through Strength people have always seemed like a lot of harmless crackpots. And that's what they were." He tapped his fingers against the desktop. "... until recently. I don't think they just suddenly transformed into a highly competent and directed worldwide movement. Someone big– in both countries– is funding them and pulling the strings in the background."

"Who?" Robert asked.

"That is what we will need you– and your Mirror-Walkers– to find out," the President replied. He looked thoughtful for a moment and then said, "My best guess would be to follow the money, but I have a feeling that they have their money paths very closely guarded. We are obviously dealing with some very powerful people. We will need to know for sure who to target before we can move."

He tapped his fingers even harder on the desk. "The problem is that I don't know who to trust. From what you say, my experts might not be loyal to me. Most of them are young idealists, and as recent exposures by Wikileaks have shown, nothing is worse than a misguided idealist or zealot. These PTS people probably have a lot of good people on their side who don't know what the true aims of that organization are. I'm sure they think it is just something like good fences make good neighbors."

Mark huffed slightly, "But it's really good nukes make good enemies."

"Exactly," said the First Lady. "That explains what they did last year. They weren't trying to start a war. They were trying to force everyone to the brink of war... and keep us there."

"That's a very dangerous game," the President said. "It's like trying to see how close you can stand to the edge of a cliff."

Mark and Robert both looked at him. He let out a heavy breath and said flatly, "The only way to find out for sure is to go too far and fall off."

He turned to Robert and asked, "What do you need from me?"

"Money and communications," Robert answered. "Lucy tells me she can get some experts of our own, but it will cost a lot of Bitcoins, whatever those are. She says she needs an account with sixty thousand dollars in Bitcoins that she can offer her hackers– I mean experts. And we need a way to access the internet and to communicate with each other without showing up on everyone's radar. We also need money for our expenses."

"Government satellite phones," Mark said. "We have some that are untraceable as long as you keep them off most of the time and don't call a high-security government number... like the White House. As far as the internet... I don't know."

Helena spoke up. "Go to a discount place," she

said calmly, "and buy a decent laptop. Pay cash. Fake the registration. Set up fake email and twitter accounts. Use it for a week or at most a month and then close the accounts. Wipe the laptop and dump it. They're cheap. Just buy another one and start all over again."

When everyone looked at her in shock, she smiled back at them and said, "No one has ever found a trace of my internet activity from before Douglas was elected– not even from during the campaign."

"Well," said Robert, "if the media and their syncopates haven't been able to backtrack you, it must work."

Helena suddenly looked over her husband's shoulder and said, "David and Chi, I want to again say 'thank you' for all that you did last year. Be assured that no one in our government will attempt to force you to do anything you don't want to do." She then looked at her husband, gave the same smile that she had given the guard, and said, "At least not while I have anything to say about it."

Robert raised his eyebrows, but said nothing.

Mark said, "I'll get those phones sent over and then take you back to the tram stop."

"Bad form, little brother," Robert said as they started to walk out of the office. "Never go back to the same spot unless you have to. Never do anything the same twice. Drop me off at Arlington Cemetery. I'll wander around with the tourists and take a few pictures and then walk over to the Metro station."

"Where are you staying?" the President asked from behind them.

Robert turned back to face him and said politely, "Where nobody will find me, sir. Where nobody will find me."

He could hear Helena laughing softly as the door closed behind him.

Robert spent several hours riding the Metro throughout the DC area before finally boarding the correct line to take him out to the last stop at Springfield, Virginia. When he got there, he walked up to a fellow passenger who looked like a tourist and said, "Could you do me a real favor? I lost my cellphone somewhere..." He dropped his voice and looked very discouraged. "... or somebody stole it while I was walking around DC. Would you please call an Uber for me so I can get back to my hotel?"

As expected, the fellow tourist was very accommodating. He even stood talking to Robert for the ten minutes it took for the Uber car to arrive. Robert had the Uber take him to the Holiday Inn in Dumfries, Virginia, one exit north on I-95 from the entrance to the park. He paid the driver and gave a standard tip. A very average tip was important because he wanted the driver to *NOT* remember him. Too much of a tip would make him stand out as much as too little. He walked into the hotel lobby and waited for the Uber to leave. Then he began walking up the path alongside Dumfries Road toward the RV park located on the north side of the Forest Preserve.

It was about two and a half miles from the hotel to the RV park where the bigger rigs and those who wanted things like water and electricity camped. It wasn't the RV park Robert wanted, however, but rather Pleasant Road, a side entrance to the Forest Preserve alongside the RV park which led to some cabins and a group camping area. A short way inside the park he turned off the blacktop road onto an old fire trail with the interesting name of "Burma Road." It continued up through the trees following the rugged contour of the land. His shoes were dusty by the time he had walked the mile and a half of rock and gravel to get to the main park roads. He was still three miles from the campground when he began walking once again on asphalt. The road was smoother, but no less hilly. He was sweating lightly by the time he finally finished his long hike to the campsite.

When he arrived, Lucy was sitting at the picnic table. "Momma Ling is inside trying to convince Chi to stay out of the mirror," she said as he approached. "Whatever she does to go mirror walking really takes it out of her."

"Yeah," he said as he set a large Smithsonian shopping bag on the table. "I saw that in David last year. He looked like death warmed over after a few days."

He then pointed to the bag and said, "I've got five satellite phones in the bag with chargers. Mark says they are untraceable if we don't use them too much and don't call the wrong people." He opened the top of the bag and added, "There is also fifty grand in cash for expenses and two credit cards for Richard Blain. We can use the cash to stop at a WalMart or Target or whatever and pick up some laptops and then use the wireless here or at whatever camp we are at."

Lucy looked up at him and said, "Who's Richard Blain?"

"Haven't you seen *ANY* of the great classic movies?" he responded in mock indignation. Then he held up a Missouri driver's license with that name and his picture on it.

Lucy just looked at him sternly and said, "Chi's been back for hours. Where have you been?"

"Did a little sightseeing on the Metro," he answered with a grin. Then he added, "... just to confuse the competition. I don't think anyone was following me. Or if they were, maybe I got lucky and lost them at one of the transfer points."

She looked up at him in shock and said, almost angrily, "You rode around on the subway in Washington, DC, for three hours with fifty grand in a paper bag!?"

"A Smithsonian bag," he said with a big smile. "Nobody's going to steal a bunch of tourist crap regardless of where I am."

He paused and then asked, "Do you think Jimmy and his friends will do it?"

"From what Chi told us," she said, "I've got sixty thousand reasons that should convince him."

"Yeah," Robert replied, "and the message is set up for tomorrow night."

"When will you call him?" he asked.

"First thing tomorrow," she replied. "Which for him would be well after noon."

Chapter Eleven
"A Little Help From a Friend"

At two o'clock the next day, Lucy put a battery into one of the burner phones and made a call. She began with her customary, "Hiya, Jimmy!" then lowered her voice and quickly followed that with "got an offer you can't refuse." She had the volume turned up so Robert, standing next to her, could hear both sides of the conversation, but neither her voice nor the phone itself was loud enough to be heard in the next campsite.

"That could mean a couple of different things," replied a wary voice. "Is that a threat or a promise?"

"Both," replied Lucy. "There could be some big money in it for you... and I really need you to do this for me."

"How much money?" Jimmy asked. "And what do I have to do?"

"Let's say we start with ten grand as a retainer with a promise of more as needed." she replied. "Money's guaranteed and untraceable. I've got a Bitcoin account that I can pull from."

"This sounds like something that could get me put away," Jimmy said, almost angrily. "You know me. I work on the edge. I don't tug on Superman's cape, if you get what I mean. I make enough to be comfortable, but everybody leaves me alone because it ain't worth their trouble to take me down."

"I understand," Lucy said sweetly, "but you would be on the right side this time. Superman would have your back and he's willing to back me for at least 60K, more if I need it. With that kind of backing, whatever you do for me would almost be like being protected by a get out of jail free card."

"How do I know you're not playing me, cop lady?" he asked. "You can promise anything now and deny it all if something goes to court." Anger was starting to show in his voice.

"Record the President's news conference tonight," she said firmly. "Watch it first thing in the morning. I will call you back tomorrow after you know whether or not I'm telling the truth."

"You mean the President of the United States?" he asked incredulously.

"Like I said," she replied, "Superman is on your side."

"You could be on my side, too," he said in a soft, almost sing-song voice.

The next thing he said was very soft and Robert couldn't hear it. Her response of "Never happen, James!" was loud enough, however, to cause heads to turn in the adjacent campsites.

After she shut off the phone, she turned to Robert and said, "Now we wait."

She looked around and asked, "Where's Ling?"

"Chi's back in the mirror," he replied. "David thinks that Ranger Rick is going to stop in this afternoon. He seems to show up on a three day and then four day schedule.

"Sounds like he checks in on Tuesdays and Fridays," Lucy said. She smiled and said, "I'll bet he has to file a written report for a Monday meeting and then take any orders from that meeting out to the guards. He's probably there today to pick up the guards' weekly reports. That sounds like government bureaucracy."

Robert laughed, "Definitely bureaucracy, but bureaucracy doesn't have to be government. David and Chi are going to follow him back to wherever it is that he's actually from."

***

Chi and David stood in the guard room watching the guards frantically fill out the forms and reports they had been ignoring for the past several days. "It looks like he will be here soon," Chi said. "He must pick up these reports and take them back somewhere."

"That somewhere is what we have to figure out," David answered. "I just hope it isn't too far away."

"Once we go to him," Chi said, "will the bubble go with us?"

"Yes," he answered, "as long as he is near a mirror. But that's not what I'm worried about. You have been in the mirror too long for too many days. I know you are there watching me even when I am not in the mirror. That's too much. I don't want you to destroy yourself trying to save me."

"I would gladly give my life for you," Chi said firmly.

"I know," David answered. "And I would also gladly give my life for you... if necessary." His voice became stern as he said, "But right now it is not necessary! You don't have to destroy yourself in order to free me. They know where I am. When the time comes, they will act."

He turned her so they were facing each other. "I want to meet you in the real world as well as in the mirror. If you destroy yourself before I am free, I will never be able to do that."

Chi lowered her eyes. "For you, I will limit my time in the mirror." She looked up with tears brimming in her eyes, "But I will always check on you each morning and each evening."

"I can stay with the ranger," David said. "You go back and rest. Go into the mirror later, but before the sun gets too low in the sky, and we will sit and talk."

Chi nodded her head and then shimmered and disappeared.

Shortly after she left, the heavy outer door squealed and the man dressed in the park ranger's uniform stepped into the guard room.

"Anything new?" he asked as he walked briskly over to the inner door and lifted the gray curtain.

"Not even anything old," the guard at the monitor station replied. "He stands looking up the vent pipe for hours and then does some exercises and then eats and then stands looking up the vent pipe. He's a nothing nerd from Iowa. I don't know what's so damn dangerous about him."

The man in the ranger uniform spun from the cell door and grabbed the guard by the back of the collar. He pulled him nearly to his feet and growled, "That nothing nerd shut down an operation it took me four years to setup. He got one of my best field men killed and nearly put my neck in a noose. Do *NOT* underestimate him! If you screw this up, I will personally feed your body to the sharks."

He let go of the guard's collar and the guard crashed to the ground. Turning to the other two guards he said loudly, "Has *ANYTHING* happened this week that was at all unusual?"

"He stopped singing so much," one of the other guards answered timidly.

"What do you mean?" the ranger asked harshly.

"He often sings to himself while he is staring up that pipe," the guard explained. "He hasn't been doing that as much lately."

"That's probably nothing," the ranger said slowly, "but make sure it's in your report."

"You want us to add that to this week's report?" the third guard asked.

"No," the ranger said, "but put it in next week if it continues."

He then took the reports from the guard's hand and

104

strode out the door. What he didn't know was that the nothing nerd from Iowa was walking right behind him. As he walked around the car to get into the driver's seat, David pushed through the passenger door and sat beside him.

David had no idea where they might be going. There wasn't anything to do but sit and wait to see where the ranger went, so he relaxed slightly and watched the waves softly washing up onto the beach as they drove east toward the park entrance. As soon as they passed the entrance, the man took off his uniform hat and removed the badge and name tag from his shirt. Obviously he wasn't a real ranger.

He was, however, most likely a real American. David became sure of that when a Mustang convertible with four young tourists in it cut them off as it pulled out from one of the rental beach homes. The man's expert use of American slang and curse words when he was alone meant American English was most likely his native language.

A few minutes after that, the ranger's cellphone rang and he reached forward and pushed something on the dash. A mechanical voice said, "Answering." He looked over at the radio and spoke one word, "Lufton."

Since the phone was operating in hands-free mode, David could clearly hear the person on the other end "Frank," the voice said, "what's going on? My people say that the brother from Iowa was at the White House."

"You sure?" Frank replied.

"Our man was ordered not to log him in," the voice said, "but it was definitely him."

"Shit!" was Frank's only comment. Then he asked, "We got eyes on him?"

"No," the voice replied. "We had him at Arlington Cemetery and followed him all over hell on the Metro, but he gave our guys the slip. He could be anywhere."

David felt himself letting out a breath he did not know he had been holding in. They still didn't know where Chi was. For now, she was still safe.

"When will you be back at the office?" asked the voice on the cellphone.

"It's two-thirty now, Mister Connor," he answered, "I'm just crossing the channel to Gulf Breeze. I should be there by five-thirty, six at the latest."

"I will be in my office," the voice said tersely. "I want to talk about our options now that the operation is approaching completion."

"He's a nice kid, Mister Connors," the false ranger said.

"But he's becoming a liability," the voice replied harshly. "If we can't neutralize the Nash brothers in the next ten days, I am afraid that we will have to abandon project mirror weapon. Everything will be in motion then anyway."

"Understood," Frank replied. He then put his phone back in his pocket and cussed softly for the next several blocks as he drove through Gulf Breeze and got onto I-110 North.

David stayed with him until the 110 merged with I-10 West. Then he whispered softly, "Chi."

To his great surprise, he ended up back in his bunker prison. Chi was sitting on his bed facing his non-mirror body as it stared up into the vent pipe. She startled when he appeared next to her. "I came here to watch over you," she said. "I was going to warn you if the guards thought something was wrong." She looked down and said softly, "I think they suspect something."

David pulled her into his arms and she cried softly on his shoulder for several minutes. He then stood back up and said, "We have to report back to Detective Nash. They know he went to the White House yesterday."

Chi gasped. Then both of them said together,

"Van."

Robert and Lucy were sitting at the picnic table when Ling stuck her head out of the van and yelled for them. As they approached, she said more quietly, "Chi says you need to both come into the van."

Robert hesitated and Ling said, "There is no time for modesty. We are all in danger."

Both Robert and Lucy unconsciously checked to see that their weapons were in place as they stepped into the van.

When the door closed, Ling said quickly, "Chi says that David is here. They know you went to the White House yesterday."

"Do they know where we are?!" Robert practically shouted as he pulled his Glock from his waist.

"No," Ling said, "you lost them on the subway."

Chi turned from the mirror. She was sobbing almost hysterically. Ling spent several minutes quieting her and then said, "Beloved tells her that they plan to kill him in ten days. There is evidently something that is planned to happen before then or shortly thereafter."

Robert said, "That'd be the end of the month or the first of next month."

Lucy moved over and held Chi as she continued to sob. Robert spoke softly to Ling. "Ask Chi what else Beloved told her."

Ling spoke softly to Chi and Chi stood and once again faced the mirror. A few minutes later she again turned toward them and spoke to Ling. Her voice was much more controlled, but she was still obviously distraught.

"Beloved says," Ling translated, "that the ranger's real name is Frank Lufton. He is driving to someplace west of Pensacola on Interstate 10 and it will take him about three hours to get there. The boss' last name might be Connors because that's who told the ranger that if the

Nash brothers weren't neutralized in the next ten days they would have to kill Beloved."

Chi said something else and Ling said, "Oh, and the spy at the White House is the man who was ordered not to log in Warrior Robert, whatever that means."

"Holy Shit!" Robert exclaimed. "One of the White House guards is on their side."

"Detective Nash," Ling said strongly, "I would appreciate it if Kong Jing did not learn certain English words from you."

"I apologize," he said, "but sometimes my mouth speaks before my brain thinks."

"You should have heard him," Lucy said with a laugh, "before I convinced him to clean up his language."

"I understand," Ling said, "but I am, in effect, Jing's mother and..."

"I also understand," Robert said, holding up his hands almost as if in surrender. "Never get between a Momma bear and her cubs."

"That is an American idiom that I do understand," Ling said firmly.

"So what now?" Robert said as he looked over at Chi standing in front of the mirror.

"David and Chi need to follow Lufton and see where he is going and who he is meeting with," Lucy said.

"Chi needs to rest," Ling said, "And David needs to come out of the mirror so he can eat. Otherwise the guards will sense a change in routine. After that it will be too dark for David to see in the mirror. Chi will have to follow Lufton."

"Did you hear that?" Robert said to the mirror. A few moments later, Chi took a deep breath and reached for her robe.

She said something to Ling in Chinese and Ling

said, "David has gone back to the bunker. Chi will rest here until five o'clock and then go to wherever Frank Lufton is."

"I need to code a message to my brother," Robert said, "and Lucy needs to sic her teenaged lover and his friends on Frank Lufton and anyone named Connors that may have crossed his path."

Lucy bristled slightly and then said, "He's twenty-seven." She softened her voice and added, "He has a crush on me, that's all."

"Which you encourage," Robert retorted.

"Anything that gets results," she answered with a smile as she dug one of the phones out of the duffle bag. A few minutes later she said, "Hiya, Jimmy. Change of plans. I need you to start this job on faith. ... and an extra ten grand."

"That doesn't sound good," Jimmy replied. "What changed?"

"One," Lucy replied, "we've got a name for you to work on, and two... ... we have a hard deadline that we have to beat."

"What's the name?" Jimmy asked.

"Frank Lufton," Lucy said. He is likely based out of New Orleans and is somehow tied in with someone named Connors."

"Not Connors Armament Connors, I hope," said Jimmy.

"And if it is?" Lucy said.

"Then we are talking at least another ten K," he responded, "... and Superman better mention me by name tonight because we are going up against the Dark Lord himself."

"Never happen, James," Lucy said lightly, "but you will absolutely know he is talking to you. I guarantee it."

"He'd better." Jimmy said.

"Watch the news conference live," Lucy said. "I'll call you when he says it."

Once again he said something too soft for anyone else to hear, and once again Lucy's very loud response was, "Never happen, James!"

***

While Chi was sleeping, Lucy was helping Robert craft three separate messages. The first said: "NEWS CONFERENCE X QUESTION MUST COME FROM JIMMY OLSEN TDW"

The second message said:

"GUARD GATE IS MOLE X NO ACTION X PICKUP SAME TOMORROW"

The third message was in clear text and said only "D-10d"

Mark Nash, with Presidential permission– actually on Presidential orders– had a personal cellphone on in his inside pocket. It wasn't his normal personal cellphone. It was one of Robert's cold burners that he had given him when he came to the White House. When it vibrated he checked for a new text. A series of eight texts carried a ten by ten grid message. After a long pause, another eight texts carried another ten grid message. It was the seventeenth message, however, which caused Mark to run down the hallway to the oval office. After a quick word with the President's personal secretary and the guards outside the office doors, he walked in and showed the President his phone.

"I haven't decoded the main message," he said, "but whatever is going to happen is going to happen in ten days."

The President looked up from the phone, "I assume that means D minus ten days. D-day is ten days from now?"

Mark nodded. "I will get back to you as soon as I have decoded the other two messages," he said.

"Just tell Helen," President Travis replied. "She will get things going on it and keep me in the loop."

Chapter Twelve
"A Devious Plan"

Robert, Lucy, and Ling sat around the picnic table talking softly until just before five. That's when Ling walked back to the van to wake Chi. She spoke to her in Chinese, "My little Chi," she said, "I know that you would do anything to save your beloved, but you must also save yourself. It will do David no good if you die and he is still captive." She stroked her granddaughter's face lightly and said, "Be careful."

"I will, Momma Ling," Chi replied as she stood in front of the mirror and began repeating softly, "Frank Lufton, Frank Lufton, Frank Lufton."

It was slightly disorienting for Chi to suddenly be in the back seat of a car doing seventy miles an hour down the interstate. She had stepped into airplanes before, but a car has windows all around and the sudden change from standing stationary to highway speed caused her to startle with fright.

Her fright faded rapidly, however, as she watched the man at the wheel. This was the man who would kill her beloved if she could not free him from his prison. She pushed herself into the front seat and began examining everything which was visible about both the car and Frank Lufton.

There was a plastic or laminated paper tag attached to the dashboard with some words and a long number on it. In front of the numbers were the letters I D. She repeated the number to herself several times and then sang it out loud to a popular Chinese children's song. She would remember it.

Her examination of Frank Lufton yielded little except the fact that he was apparently trying to quit smoking. There was a package of nicotine patches sitting on the seat next to him. He was also smoking, however, which indicated either that he didn't have much willpower or that something was putting him under a great deal of stress. Perhaps both were correct.

Chi tried to read the green interstate signs as they passed them. She knew the numbers were in miles and that most likely the words were the names of towns. She recognized one town, New Orleans, because she had always wanted to visit there and see what Mardi Gras was really like. She also recognized the word "Exit." The sign said, "New Orleans next 5 exits."

Frank stayed on I-10 until he exited onto a road named something 90. Chi was awestruck at the many tall buildings. It was not that she hadn't seen big cities before, but she had always pictured all of New Orleans to be like the images of the French Quarter which she had looked at so often when dreaming about going to Mardi Gras someday.

Chi had no idea for sure where she was when Frank turned suddenly into a car park and moved rapidly up the ramp to at least the sixth level. This was apparently the highest parking floor because the ramps ended here and the rest of the floor was level. Chi looked around for anything which would identify the building as he pulled into a reserved spot near the elevators and shut off the car. She was surprised that he didn't press the button to call an elevator, but instead put a key in a special plate near the last elevator. A few moments later, the doors opened and he stepped in.

There were no buttons in this elevator, only a series of key switches with no numbers next to them. In place of numbers there were small colored circles, evidently to make it easier for someone to remember which switch to use. Frank put his key in the fourth switch from the top– the green one– and turned it. The elevator began moving immediately. The indicator above the door counted up to nine before the doors opened.

Frank walked briskly through an open area past a woman sitting at a desk. He nodded at her but neither said anything until he reached a door with a keypad lock of some sort next to it. She then said "two fifteen." Before Chi could get into position to see his hands, he punched a long string of numbers into the keypad and stepped into another receptionist area. Again, without saying a word– and this time not even nodding to the woman at the desk– he moved through that area into a large office. Once inside, with the door closed behind him, he opened a closet and began to change clothes. Chi stood watching as he disrobed, primarily to see if he had any tattoos or other identifying marks.

There were no tattoos, but there were two small, flat knives, one on his left arm and one on his right shin. There was also a very small gun high on his back between his shoulder blades. As he was changing, he suddenly spun around and looked behind himself. His hand was up at the back of his neck, grasping the gun.

"Getting touchy in my old age," he said quietly to himself, "but things are about to get real, and when it does who knows what will happen."

Chi smiled. She knew that what he had felt was her glowering at him. She continued to scowl at him as he slowly dressed in a very fashionable suit and tie. He no longer looked like a park ranger. Now he looked like a very successful business executive, which, in a way, he was.

He looked over at a pile of papers on his desk and grimaced. "Paperwork, paperwork, paperwork," he muttered angrily to himself. "Oh, how I yearn for the good old days when all a mercenary needed was a gun and an army."

He sat down and picked up an old-fashioned telephone handset mounted on the side corner of his desk. He waited a short while and then said simply, "Lufton." After a moment he nodded and hung the handset back in its holder. As he reached out and moved the mouse on his desktop, he continued his angry tirade, "And I'll bet this is only half of it. I wonder what great ideas came into Everett's head today."

He made a few more grumbling noises as he logged into the computer and then onto the internal network. Once everything came up, he settled down to work on the items on his desk.

Chi had tried to read his first password over his shoulder, but all that appeared on the screen were asterisks. She tried to watch as he typed on the keyboard for the second password, but was not able to accurately follow his fingers as he typed rapidly. Turning away from the desk, she walked around Lufton's office examining everything that she could see before shimmering and disappearing.

Several minutes later, Ling stepped out of the van and returned to Robert and Lucy who were eating sandwiches at the picnic table. She set a small notebook on the table and said, "Chi is very tired. I told her she can listen to what we have to say for a short while and then she must sleep."

She looked down at the notebook and began reading, "Frank Lufton drove to an office building in New Orleans. It is near a highway with a 90 in its name. The building itself appears to have twelve floors because his office is on the ninth floor and there were three more locks above that. The first five or six floors are partially or wholly a car park."

She glanced up and said, "Evidently there is an express elevator that is key operated. Chi says that he used a key rather than pushing buttons to call the elevator and then to select his floor. Chi was not able to discern the code to open his office door or his passwords as he signed into his computer. The code to open the door was long and appeared to be all numbers. The password was about the same length, perhaps no more than a dozen characters."

She then looked back at her notebook. "Frank Lufton has no tattoos or other marks on his body, but does carry two throwing knives and a gun. The knives are on his left forearm and his right shin. The gun is high on his back so he can reach it from behind his neck. He spoke of being a mercenary and of having had armies in the past. He also complained that someone named Everett kept coming up with new ideas."

She closed the notebook, looked up, and said something in Chinese. "I told Chi she should go back to the van now," Ling explained.

"Wait a minute," Robert said quickly. "I know this is asking a lot, but I need Chi to go back into the mirror later tonight... say around ten. Do you think she will be able to do that?"

Ling looked at him with a frown on her face. "Now that she has heard you say it," she said dryly, "there is no way that I will be able to stop her."

Robert tried to smile back at her in an apologetic sort of way, but he knew he had once again stepped between a Momma bear and her cub.

***

It was nearly ten o'clock when Robert knocked on the side door of the van. "Ling," he said softly, "is Chi up and decent? I would like to talk to her."

The door slid open and Robert and Lucy stepped inside.

"Does Chi need to go into the mirror for you to explain what you need?" Ling asked.

"No," Robert answered. "It might even be best if

116

you translated this so that the mirror doesn't change anything."

Ling nodded and he began. "First off," he said, "I need to know if a name and picture are absolutely needed or is it possible to go to someone based on just their name?"

Ling translated the question and the answer. "Chi says," she answered, "that the picture is needed because many people may have the same name. Somehow the picture helps the Mirror-Walker go to the correct person with that name. If she has seen the person before and remembers their face, no picture is needed, but otherwise, yes, she needs a picture of the person."

Robert nodded. "But what if," he asked, "the name was so unique that there was only one person in the entire world with that name?"

After a moment, Ling responded, "Chi doubts that such a name exists, but she says that in that case, the mirror would probably take her to that person."

Robert smiled widely and set a piece of paper on the small table. "I need Chi to go to this person," he said. "I need her to tell me things about him that no one could possibly know. I want to be able to prove to him that we were in his house, in his room, standing there alongside him tonight and, if possible, tomorrow morning. I want him to think that we are everywhere. I want to make him more afraid of us than of whomever it is that he actually works for."

Ling smiled up at him. "You are a very devious man, Detective Nash," she said. "I think my late husband would have enjoyed working with you."

Robert remained silent. Partly that was to allow Ling to translate his request to Chi but mostly it was because he wasn't sure if he had just be complimented... or insulted... or warned... or possibly all three.

After a moment, Ling turned to Robert and said,

"If you will now give us some privacy."

He murmured, "Thank you," and he and Lucy stepped back out of the van.

"What are you doing?" she asked in a hushed whisper as soon as the door closed.

Robert grinned at her and said, "Room 101."

"What?" she replied.

"Have you ever read 1984 or seen the movie?" he asked.

She stood still for a moment, obviously thinking. Then she said simply, "Oh."

***

The next day, Robert had Lucy drive him to the Metro station in Vienna, Virginia. It was about twenty miles farther than the Springfield station, but he didn't want to use the same Metro line to go into the city. He knew it was a risk, but he went a second time to the Jefferson Memorial. At noon, his brother Mark pulled up in a small sports car.

"I thought using one of the SUVs might be repeating myself," he said as his brother squeezed into the passenger seat.

"You're learning," Robert replied with a smile, "but I thought I explained things in the followup messages. It would have been better if we had the SUV or at least a four-door.

"How 'bout a van with doors on both sides?" he asked as he turned down a side street and into a parking garage. There was an empty space on the third floor right next to a large, black van. The space was empty because two people were standing in it apparently trying to make sense of a map of the city.

When Mark pulled up, they stepped aside and let him enter. "Only had to wave a dozen people off," the woman said. "Most were OK with us saying that we were saving this spot for our son."

"One jerk was going to push past us," the man said somewhat harshly, "but I convinced him it would be better if he parked on the next level."

"Nothing official?" Mark asked.

"No," the man said. "I just growled at him a little... and wrinkled his tie a bit... ... when I pulled it up over his head."

Robert chuckled. "Local talent?" he asked his brother.

"Undercover Secret Service," Mark answered. "Normally they blend in with the crowds to spot anything we can't see from up front. I've worked with them for several years. I know them and I'm sure of them."

"OK," Robert answered as he got out of the car.

"All of you need to ride in the back," his brother said. "I got your additional messages and everything is set up."

As he got in, the woman, who had already seated herself in the back, smiled at him and said, "Good to meet you, Detective Nash. I like your plan. Remind me not to ever really piss you off. You scare me and I've seen a lot in this job."

"Learned it all from my little brother," Robert said with a laugh.

***

A short while later, the black van was at the entrance to the White House parking area. "I've got to look inside the van, Mark," the guard said. "Is the side door unlocked?"

Mark nodded and the guard slid the door open. As soon as the door opened, he stiffened and then stood there with his mouth slightly agape and his hand twitching nervously on the butt of the weapon at his side. From inside the van, two weapons with silencers attached were aimed directly at him. Both had laser sights and a quick glance told him that one red dot was right over his heart. He had no doubt that the second dot was in the center of his forehead.

"We know you are a mole, Otis," Mark said softly. "You have a big decision to make right now. You can get into the van very quietly or you can die where you stand."

Another voice came from inside the van, "Either way, Otis," the voice said, "no one will ever know you're gone."

The person speaking moved slightly forward. He was wearing a White House guard's uniform... and Otis' face. An extremely realistic latex mask made him look almost exactly like the guard standing outside the van.

"You step in," the man said evenly. "I step out."

The guard stared into the van. He was still nervously gripping the service weapon on his hip.

"If we have to drop you," the man said evenly, "I will step out and take your place. Then in about twenty minutes, I will ask to be relieved because of severe stomach flu. It will get worse. Tomorrow I will go to the hospital but the doctors will be unable to save me."

He smiled at the trembling guard and said, "The Director of the Secret Service will send flowers for your funeral."

The guard let his hands fall to his side and ducked his head to step into the van. As soon as he stepped in, his doppelganger was stepping out. "Nothing on the prohibited list inside, Mark," the replacement guard said loudly as he returned to his post. As he slid the side door back closed, he added, "I hate vans with no windows. I'm getting too old to keep getting in and out of things like this. ... and I'll have to do it again when you leave."

Mark just nodded his head and drove on into the underground parking area. The two additional agents remained in the van while Mark, Robert, and Otis walked to a secure room another level down. The room was evidently used for meetings or planning or something like that because there was a large table with a dozen or so chairs surrounding it. The walls held white boards and video screens, but they were all blank. As soon as the three men entered the room, Mark whispered something to Robert and walked back out.

Robert positioned the guard in the middle of the table on one side and spoke softly to him. "You will keep your hands on the table at all times," he said in a very firm voice. "We've unloaded your weapon, but if you move your hands, I will assume you are trying something and will double tap your forehead. You got that?"

Otis slowly nodded his head. He had no doubt that Robert could put two bullets in his head at this range and Robert's eyes boring through him made it clear that he would not hesitate to do exactly as he said.

A few moments later, the guard gasped loudly as Mark and President Travis entered the room. Despite the warning, he shot to his feet and stood at attention. When he realized what he had done, he looked over at Robert in fear. The President, however, merely looked at him and said politely, "Please, be seated." The guard sat back down, remembering to place his hands on the tabletop. Robert sat at the table next to him. Mark and the President were on the other side with the President now directly across the table from him.

"I need you to tell me," the President began, "everything you know about the Peace Through Strength movement."

The guard startled slightly but immediately said,

"I'm sorry, sir, I don't know what you mean."

"I know all about you, Mister Mayberry," the President said flatly as he looked down at a paper he had set on the table. "I know that you had a terrible time in your childhood with everyone teasing you about your first name."

He smiled and said almost angrily, "What kind of parents with a last name of Mayberry would name a child Otis?" He paused and then said with obvious disgust, "Otis Mayberry? Otis was the old drunken fool!"

He looked the guard in the eyes. "Perhaps that name is why you joined Peace Through Strength," he said. "Or perhaps it was because you have a bright red, heart-shaped birthmark in the middle of your chest that made it hell to shower in gym class. "

The guard's eyes were wide open.

"Oh yes," the President said firmly. "We know about the birthmark even though you neglected to mention it in your pre-employment workups. We also know about the girlfriend's name you had tattooed on your right hip and then tried to have removed. Laser removal is pretty good, but you can still just barely read 'Elain' when you first come out of the shower in the morning and your skin is still all warm."

The guard's eyes were now starting to dart nervously around the room.

"We also know that each evening you take all of the change out of your pocket and put it in a jar on your dresser– actually two jars, one for the pennies and one for the larger change."

The President paused and looked up at Otis. "Last night," he continued, "it was sixty-three cents. We know that last night you wore blue and white pajamas to bed and that right now you are wearing grey boxers under your uniform pants. They have a tear on the right side and you almost threw them away this morning, but decided to wear them one last time. We know that last night you made yourself a cup of hot tea just before going to bed, which, judging from the stack of tea boxes on your kitchen counter, you evidently do quite often."

The President leaned forward across the table. His voice became very, very hard as he whispered harshly, "I have loyal people on my staff, Mister Mayberry, who know a thousand untraceable poisons."

The guard's eyes were now still, but very wide.

The President sat back into his chair and looked at him in silence. After what seemed like forever to Otis Mayberry, he said softly, "So, the question I need to answer is, 'Do I use you as an asset or neutralize you as a threat?'"

Douglas Travis then smiled at Otis Mayberry. Nothing he had said to that point created more terror than that smile. The President's face would have looked good in a newspaper picture taken from a distance, but up close, the top of his face, and especially his eyes were devoid of all emotion. It was not a smile at all. It was a wolf baring his fangs at an enemy. In that instant, the guard knew absolutely that no one could help him. If he refused to cooperate, he would not leave this room alive.

His shoulders slumped. "What do you need?" he asked nervously.

Chapter Thirteen
"Superman and Jimmy"

At seven o'clock Robert, Lucy, Ling, and Chi crowded into David's van. Robert had started the engine to charge the camping batteries while they sat watching the small television set which was mounted above the bed. The picture kept breaking up and pixelating, but it was sufficient to watch the special report on the presidential news conference.

The news conference itself was mostly the standard sparring between the President and the press. Surprisingly, Douglas Travis was not as loose and natural as he normally was. And even more surprisingly, he took questions from a few of his staunch opponents in the press whom he normally annoyed by avoiding. Then, near the end of the press conference, he held up a small notepad computer.

"When I was elected," he said loudly, "I promised that I would take questions from all news sources. But it has been brought to my attention that we seem to have been ignoring the vast newsweb out there. So, my staff has pre-screened three web news agencies to allow them to submit questions."

The first two questions were actually from news aggregators which most people recognized. The third question, however, was from The Daily Web. None of the reporters had ever heard of it– primarily because it didn't exist.

"Jimmy Olsen of The Daily Web," the President said, reading from his notepad, "is asking me what the most unusual thing is that I have had to do so far as President."

He chuckled. "Jimmy," he began, "I have to be honest and say that there is a lot that the President does that you know nothing about until you are sitting behind that desk in the oval office, but I think something that I did today was very unexpected by me." He chuckled again. "Today I had to authorize putting sixty thousand dollars into a Bitcoin account so that we could anonymously pay an... um... outside consultant... for some rather specialized work on the internet." He laughed and shook his head. "Obviously, I'm not going to say what that work is, but I will tell you, Jimmy, that I authorized it personally because it is vital to our national interests and the defense of this nation."

The President then looked out over the gathered news people and said, "Thank you all for coming. That is all for today." There were the standard shouted questions as the President left the podium, and as usual, he ignored them.

As soon as the President finished, Lucy was putting the battery back in the cellphone.

"Hiya, Jimmy," she said brightly. "I hope you recorded that because the President just told the world that he is authorizing what you are doing and it is vital to the national interests and defense of the nation."

Her voice got louder as she said, "That, Jimmy boy, is a *Get out of Jail Free* card." Her voice got harder and even louder as she added, "... as long as you stick to just what we tell you to do! No slipping something else in and hoping it is protected!"

She had the volume turned way down on her phone so Robert couldn't hear the response.

"Yes," she said. "The names are Frank Lufton and Everett Connors. We need to know what they are up to and who all is involved."

She listened quietly for a few moments and then said with a slight laugh, "Never happen, Jimmy." After a pause she said more seriously, "Jimmy, this is some serious shit. You aren't hacking into some website to change your account balance to zero. These are serious players with computer experts of their own. If they catch you, they will kill you." She paused again. There was a quiver in her voice as she said, "Be careful, Jimmy." She made a slight kissing sound into the phone before ending the call and taking out the battery.

"You care for him," Robert said softly.

"He's a sweet kid," she answered. "I'd hate to see something happen to him."

Robert started to say something else but was cut short by a very loud noise that seemed to rock the van and caused him to put his hand on his Glock and slip out the door to look around. A column of smoke and fire was rising into the sky to the southeast. A few minutes later, he leaned back in and said, "Looks like an explosion up by the highway."

A man in the next site was walking over to his pickup truck. He called over to Robert, "Want to go up and see what it is?"

Robert looked around and then again leaned into the van and grabbed his camera, "Keep sharp," he said. "This is probably an accident on the highway or something, but you never know."

About forty-five minutes later the pickup truck returned. Robert stood talking with the man in front of his tent for several minutes and then returned to the van.

"Propane or gas explosion in one of the camper units in the RV park on Dumfries Road," he said as he sat down at the small table. "At least that's what they told us."

Lucy looked over and him and said, "But?"

"I walked in as far as I could," he answered, "and then used the telephoto lens on my camera to see what was going on. I could clearly see the RV... or what was left of it. That was a high velocity explosion. It tore that van into small pieces and shredded the sides of the big RVs on either side of it. A propane or gasoline explosion wouldn't have torn up the metal like that. It would have shattered the glass and ballooned the van, not blown it all apart. Someone stuck a bomb– a big bomb– under or in that van."

"Was anyone hurt?" Ling asked.

"A couple and their teen-aged daughter were killed instantly," he said glumly. "The RV on one side was empty. The woman in the other has burns and shrapnel. A couple other campers have some minor stuff from helping get her out of her unit." He started to say something else, but instead fell silent.

"There is more," Ling said softly.

"Yes," Robert said with a sigh. "There is more. The van was from Iowa. The wife was Asian."

Lucy gasped and then said, "It was supposed to be us!"

"Yes," Robert said grimly. "It was supposed to be us. I know they didn't follow me on the subway. I was sure that I lost them. But somehow they knew we were out here."

Ling was translating for Chi. "You probably did lose them," she said. "Chi said that Uber logs are available to law enforcement without a warrant. All they had to do was look for Uber rides from the end of the subway lines."

"Damn!" Robert said. "I didn't think of that! Two rides from the end of Metro to the Dumfries Holiday Inn. I might as well have drawn an arrow on a map."

"They probably didn't know about the back entrance," Ling said. "And even if they did, they probably didn't think you would walk seven miles back to camp."

"Plus we currently have New Jersey tags on the van," Lucy added. She paused before saying very softly, "And there was someone in the RV park by the highway that matched our description, so they stopped looking."

"Yes," Robert said almost angrily, "they looked like us... and it got them killed,"

"We need to leave immediately," Ling said.

"NO!" Robert almost shouted. Then he took a deep breath and said much more calmly, "No. We need to stay at least until tomorrow. If we leave now we will draw attention to ourselves. For now, let them think they got us. We leave tomorrow around noon, the regular checkout time. Then at least those poor people will not have died in vain."

After a very long silence, he said, "There is nothing else we can do tonight. We might as well just go to bed."

Before he crawled into his tent, he put the battery in one of the burner phones and sent a clear text message to his brother. All it said was "Safe." Mark would know what it meant when he watched the news the next morning.

Chapter Fourteen
"The Black Hole"

The next morning Chi checked in with David, or to be more accurate, David checked in with her. It was around ten when Ling stuck her head out of the van and said simply, "He's here."

Robert and Lucy sat at the picnic table and spoke softly. There was a blanket on the bench opposite them, but they had no way of knowing for sure where Chi and David actually were.

"We're running out of time," Robert said, "and Connors seems to be the key. We have to risk coming up onto the grid slightly. I'm going to use the Richard Blain identity and make a reservation in a campground near New Orleans. Before we go, I'll drive over to one of the trailheads and hope there is no one in the parking area. I'll switch license plates and then we head back south. We have to find out what they're up to, and we have to know for sure if Connors is truly "the boss" or just someone high up."

He pointed at one end of the blanket, "David," he said, "while we're on the road, I want you to spend some time with Frank Lufton. I don't know how your bubble works, but if you could see what all is in those locked-off top floors of that office building it would be really helpful."

Looking at the other end of the blanket, he continued, "Report back through Chi and she can take the night shift, if needed."

David and Chi, sitting exactly opposite of where Robert had been indicating, both laughed slightly but nodded their heads.

"We'll leave at noon with the rest of the campers checking out," he said, looking at his watch. "It's about a sixteen-hour drive to New Orleans from here. With a couple of rest stops that should put us in there mid-afternoon tomorrow. Hopefully cop lady's lover boy will have found out something by then." He took a really deep breath and then said flatly, "We are absolutely playing it by ear from here on out, but we have to be really careful. I don't want to get any more innocent people killed."

***

The drive to New Orleans was long and grueling, but uneventful. Chi spent much of the first day– or at least as much as Momma Ling would allow– in the mirror. As soon as they left camp, she and David began their morning by paying a visit to Frank Lufton in his office. They appeared behind him just as he was hanging up the old-style phone and turning to log onto his computer. David watched his fingers carefully as he entered his password. He was very surprised that Frank used the same simple password both for his computer itself and also to access the office network. The password was "Operation_TOP."

Perhaps Frank was comfortable with a less that optimum password because the office network was hardwired and hack-proof. There were no Wi-Fi access points in the entire office building. The building itself was radio-shielded. No electronic signals could enter or leave the office areas. That meant that radios, televisions, and especially cellphones, would not operate in the building. There was a cable TV which came into the building, but it terminated in a special series of amplifiers which did not allow any signals to go back out through the cable.

There was an internal radio system so that the guards could communicate among themselves. Certain specially-modified cellphones could also connect to each other– or the outside world– through that heavily firewalled system. Frank Lufton and, of course, Everett Connors, had one of those type of cellphones.

It was Jimmy who informed Lucy of the security system in place on the computer network. "I've never seen anything like this, cop lady," he said when she checked with him. "There are two totally isolated networks in the building. One is a regular business network for the many subsidiaries of Connors Armaments. The other is... a dark hole."

He laughed slightly and said, "The boys and I have mirrored everything that is on the open network and have started looking through it for anything useful."

He laughed again and said, "Some idiot left a copy of the training manual for the guards down in a temporary folder on the open network. It describes the other system, and, cop lady, that system is totally hack proof. The only way to access the internal network is to call a particular guard station on a special internal telephone and ask him to connect you. That is the only thing that guard can do on the network. He's got one job and he does it right. He knows which phone is calling, so you can't fake it from the outside. Voice recognition software confirms the caller's identity. Even if we could fake that, the special phone system is some old-style thing with no electronics, so it can't be hacked either. It's all relays and stuff like that. The only way to get onto that system is to be inside one of the offices."

"Connors has to have a way to access that network when he isn't in the building," Lucy said firmly. "There has to be a way in from the outside."

"Not sure on that one, cop lady," Jimmy replied, "but we think we know how he does it. Or at least we have a good guess because from the Google Earth pictures, there is one humongous microwave horn on the roof of that building. Nobody uses those things anymore unless they are trying to send a highly-focused, very narrow beam a long distance. There must be a private microwave system of some sort that connects all of Connors' buildings and facilities. There might be a larger network that is connected through those special antennas, but again, unless you were inside one of the buildings or up in the air directly in line with the antennas, there's no way to get in. Given enough time, Government Big Ears might be able to intercept the signal and break the encryption on the microwave, but there's no way we can do it... not in just a few days."

"OK," Lucy said. "What can you tell me about Lufton and Connors and what they might be up to?"

"Connors seems like a regular business man," Jimmy began. "He's a little more ruthless than most businessmen, a little richer than most CEOs, and way more paranoid than anybody I've ever seen. He is even more paranoid than me and my friends – not quite Howard Hughes, but close. He has an active security force that could take on a small army. Since he runs Connors Armaments, they're probably better-equipped than most armies, too."

He paused and then continued, "Lufton has been working for him exclusively for about five years, maybe longer. He's a very professional mercenary with a long history in various wars all around the world. He's always on the winning side and they win because he's on their side. He doesn't have much of an electronic trail except that he follows Soldier of Fortune Magazine on Facebook and has posted there a couple of times seeking recruits for some special operation that he gives no details about."

After a long pause he added apologetically, "Sorry, cop lady, that's all I've got so far."

"Don't worry, Jimmy," Lucy said, "you're earning your money. I'll check back with you this same time tomorrow." She paused and then said softly. "Be careful," before ending the call.

***

David and Chi attempted to explore the rest of the Connors Office Building, but were only able to go as far as the mirror bubble allowed. Since Chi had been in Frank's car and followed him up in the elevator, she was able to return to those areas, and David was able to accompany her. But the rest of the building remained obscured by the mists.

At one point, they came upon a guard in the elevator and followed him for almost two hours hoping he would take them onto the other floors, but to no avail. When he wasn't sitting with another guard on the ground floor, he was riding the elevators, usually to check the parking areas. About every thirty minutes, he went to the top floor but did not get out when the elevator doors opened. Instead, he merely looked through the open doors at the receptionist who sat in a small lobby. He would ask, "OK?" and she would answer, "Yes," without even looking up from her desk. He would then wait for the door to close and proceed to the next floor. Jimmy had told them about this. According to the guard manual, any answer other than "Yes"– even "Good" or "OK"– would trigger a total building lockdown.

"Why can't that guard, Jayden, get off on at least one floor," David complained after several trips in the elevator. "The bubble barely reaches the receptionist's desk. Don't those floors need a guard?"

"You are thinking like a man," Chi replied.

"I am a man," David replied in frustration, trying to keep the anger out of his voice. "What am I missing?"

"You are assuming that a woman sitting at a lobby

desk is just a receptionist," Chi replied. "I think she IS a guard... and probably a better-armed and better-trained guard than the visible security people. It would be very difficult for someone to get past her. If Warrior Robert wants to get into one of these offices, it will have to be at night when the receptionist-guards are gone."

"We need to know what is going on the other side of those receptionists... or beautiful guards or whatever they are," David told her. "We have to get inside those other offices."

He gave a deep sigh and said, "If we only had a name and picture of someone on each floor, we would have access to the whole building. Maybe Lucy's hackers can get a name, but I doubt they can get a picture."

Chi looked at him with a smile on her face and said, "Otis Mayberry."

"What?" he sputtered.

"The guard at the presidential palace was named Otis Mayberry. I was able to go to his house without a picture because his name was unique," she explained rapidly. "If there is someone on each floor with a unique name, we would not need the picture."

"The name itself doesn't have to be that unique," David said. "If we know their job title, it can just be something like 'Bob, the vice president on the seventh floor' and we can go to him while he's at work."

Chi was again smiling. "Is there anything more unique in America," she said softly, "than a woman who is both a receptionist and a guard?"

David smiled back at her as she said, "I will go back and ask Warrior Lucy if her lover can find out the names of the receptionist-guards on each floor. If he can, then first thing tomorrow we start exploring the individual floors."

***

"Hiya, Jimmy," Lucy said cheerily a short while later. "We have a special request. Can you get us the names of the receptionists on each floor of the Connor Building?"

"No can do, cop lady," he immediately replied. "I told you that building is a black hole. We looked at the data dump we got from the regular system and it is all about Connors' businesses everywhere in the world except New Orleans. That building isn't mentioned anywhere. There is also no mention of Frank Lufton in that data. I had to get anything we have on him from other sources. Everything for that building must be behind those unbreakable firewalls."

"We really need those names, Jimmy," Lucy continued. "Are you the hacker who put graffiti on the CIA's webpage or not? You're the best, Jimmy. You can do this."

"I'll try to think of something," he replied slowly. "But this man is beyond paranoid. There are layers behind layers behind layers of protection on everything. Like I said, it's a black hole. No information comes out anywhere."

"You'll find a way," Lucy said, "If you do get anything, call me." She then gave him the number of one of the satellite phones. "I will leave that phone on," she said. "It's an untraceable government satellite phone that's never been used before."

"Everything's traceable, cop lady," Jimmy replied.

"That's why you are the only one with that phone number," Lucy answered emphatically. "Don't give it to anyone else, and don't call unless you have something."

"Maybe I could use it to call and ask you for a date," Jimmy said.

"Never happen, Jimmy," Lucy said softly. Then

even more softly she added, "Be careful," and ended the call.

***

It was starting to get dark when the satellite phone rang. Robert was driving. Ling was asleep in the passenger seat. Lucy was in the back of the van, lying on the bed next to the sleeping Chi, trying to get a little rest. She grabbed the phone out of its charger stand and said– a bit louder than she had intended– "Whadda ya got, Jimmy?"

"It's a good thing I watch those science shows on television, cop lady," he replied smoothly.

"What do you mean?" she answered.

"I got to thinking about that building being a black hole..." he said. Then he paused before asking, "Do you know how scientists measure how big a black hole actually is?"

"No, Jimmy, I don't," Lucy answered softly. "And what does that have to do with what I need?"

"They measure black holes by looking at all the stuff that the black hole sucks into it," Jimmy answered.

"...and..." Lucy replied. Her frustration was starting to show in her voice.

"That big black hole of a building sucks in a lot of stuff," Jimmy explained, "... especially around noon."

"Take-out deliveries!" Lucy said excitedly. Practically shouting, she continued, "They have to have a name to know who ordered it and where to deliver it."

"And because of the security in that building," Jimmy continued, "everything goes through the front receptionist on each floor."

He paused for effect and then said smugly, "I hacked into every restaurant and deli in a fifteen block area around the building. I have the names and credit card numbers of every customer they've had from that address in the past year."

"Jimmy," Lucy said harshly, "I told you to stick to what we needed!"

"You may need that other stuff later, cop lady," Jimmy said defensively. "I won't use the numbers... or sell them."

"You'd better not, Jimmy," Lucy said. "Superman's got a really nasty temper if you cross him."

"Can you get to the internet?" Jimmy asked. "Like to pull something from a dropbox?"

"I can't touch my accounts," Lucy said. "We're trying to stay below the radar."

"OK," Jimmy replied. "But you can get to the internet, right?"

When Lucy said, "Yes," he asked, "You got something to write with?"

Lucy answered "yes" again and he gave her the user name and password for a yahoo email account. "The list of names will be an attachment to an email in the drafts folder," he told her. "That used to be a way to avoid big brother's spy and sniff techniques, but they caught on so nobody uses it anymore. But as long as I don't use any of the magic words they won't tag the account for review and go snooping too deep."

"You're paranoid, Jimmy," Lucy said with a laugh.

"And you're naive, cop lady," he replied. "We'd make a really good couple."

He started to say something else, but Lucy cut him off with a loud, "Never happen, James!" and ended the call.

When she looked up, the van was pulled to the side of the road and Robert and Ling were staring at her. Chi was still snoring lightly on the bed beside her.

"When Chi wakes up," she said firmly, "tell her

137

we have some names." Then she added, "And tell her to get a lot of rest tonight. She and David will be busy tomorrow."

Chapter Fifteen
"A Busy Morning"

Chi wanted to start as soon as she heard about the list, but her grandmother convinced her to wait until David could go into the mirror with her. That way, they would know what was written down on the desks, walls, etc. It was therefore a little after ten when she stood swaying in the back of the van and tried to go into the mirror. Despite the fact that Robert had rigged some ropes through the roof supports that she could cling to, it was difficult for her to balance herself while at the same time relaxing enough for the tug of the mirror to pull her to David.

When she went into the mirror whispering "David... David... David..." she was surprised to find herself back in the van standing behind her non-mirror self.

"Is that what I look like while I'm in the mirror?" she asked as she looked at herself from behind.

"I think you're cute," David replied. He immediately sputtered and said, "I mean your face..." He was standing next to her and had the same view that she did. She noted that as she felt a flush of warmth, a blush appeared on her non-mirror self.

"Does your body always react to what is happening in the mirror?" she asked.

"I'm not sure," he replied. "We'll have to investigate that sometime when there aren't more pressing matters at hand."

"We have names," Chi said quickly. "Momma Ling said that there would be a list on the table."

"I see it," David said. "I think we should start with the big boss' office and see what he's up to."

He pointed down at a name on the list and said, "That says, 'Donna Furgeson, twelfth floor receptionist-guard." They both began softly repeating that name and a few moments later were standing in the reception area on the twelfth floor.

"I wonder if we can push through the wall into the main area?" David mused.

In response, Chi stepped up to– and through– the door that separated the office from the reception area. "That is not a wooden door," she said as David joined her. "It is as hard to push through as the door on your cell."

"It probably locks even tighter, too," David replied.

He spent a few moments examining the large keypad next to the doorway. "I assume this turns the alarm on and off," he said. "But I have no idea what the code is."

"Maybe it just unlocks the door," Chi said.

"We are about to find out," David said as he stepped aside to allow a secretary from the office to step up to the pad. David watched as the man keyed in what seemed to be a very long number.

"How can they remember such a long number?" he asked aloud.

"It's just the date with four more numbers," Chi answered. "The first four numbers were the year, then two for the month and two for the day, American style. All they have to remember are the last four numbers which were '1037.' It probably automatically changes each day."

"That's the time!" David said excitedly. "There's a clock above the door. You enter the year, month, day, hour, and minute to open the door."

"But the clock is wrong," Chi said. "It is five minutes slow."

"You can't get in unless you know what time is on that clock," David said. "That's what changes." He shook his head slightly and continued, "Whoever set this up was brilliant. It's simple and complex at the same time. Even if you know how the code is generated, you don't know how far off the timestamp actually is. I'll bet it alarms after you fail two or three times."

"I will bet it alarms if you fail once," Chi said emphatically.

They then both pushed their way back out into the reception area to watch the secretary return. There was another small clock directly above the door on the outside. This one was displaying the correct time. The number the man entered, however, was five minutes fast, rather than five minutes slow.

"It just keeps getting better," David marveled. "One side is the mirror of the other. I'll bet every door in the building is keyed to a slightly different offset. All you need is the time offset for that floor and you're in."

"Let us see if the Evil One is in his office," Chi said as she pushed back into the office area.

"Did you intend to call Mister Connors the Evil One or did the mirror change something?" David asked.

"I said what I meant," Chi answered harshly. "He is the one who wants you dead."

David stopped for a moment and looked at her intently.

"What is the matter?" she asked.

"For a minute there," he replied, "you looked different. You were... darker or something. The actual color of your skin didn't change, it was more like all light was gone from your face"

She looked down at the floor as if in shame and then said almost in a whisper, "Grandfather said that hate colors you in the mirror. He also said that love shows as light." She looked at the floor once again and said, "I am sorry that I let hatred color me... but Mister Connors is evil."

She smiled up at him and the darkness faded from her face.

"Well, let's see what the Grinch is up to," he said as he moved further into the office.

Chi stopped suddenly. Her eyes showed her fear. "I cannot go further," she said. Her voice was shaking slightly. "I am at the edge of the barrier."

"You need to think of me," he said. "I evidently have a bigger bubble. Think of me and you can move where I move."

Chi closed her eyes for a moment. Her face showed her concentration. Then she relaxed and walked forward to join David.

"We are in Mister Connors' office," David said. "Now you can return here or, if you think of this place, you can move about this entire room."

No one was in the office as David and Chi walked around carefully examining the desk, bookshelves, tabletops, pictures on the wall, and anything else that might give them a clue to what was going on. Most of the pictures and paintings on the wall were relatively modern except one. On the wall opposite the desk, where Mister Connors could see it while he was seated there, was what appeared to be a copy of a very old painting. Beneath it was a small, brass plaque which read "Hercules and the Hydra, Antonio del Pollaiuolo, c1475."

"There is something special about that painting," Chi said, pointing at it and then at the desk. "It is out of place in this office; it is larger than the other paintings; and it is placed where he can see it whenever he looks up from his desk. That painting is very important to him."

"I agree," David said, also nodding his head. "But what does it mean?"

"It is also the background image on his computer,"

Chi said as she walked around behind the desk.

She gasped loudly as Everett Connors stepped through her to sit down. He startled and looked around the room. She said, almost sobbing, "I did not see him come in. He felt... cold... as he passed through me."

"He sensed you," David said. "Hopefully, he didn't sense what you were thinking... or what you know."

"Can he do that?" Chi asked.

"The army guard last year," David said softly, "saw flashes of what I was thinking about."

"Then he knows I hate him," Chi said coldly.

"I doubt that will worry him," David replied. "I think he knows that a lot of people hate him and doesn't care. He is the type of person that no one really wants as a friend but has people around him because everyone is afraid to have him as an enemy."

Mister Connors, meanwhile, had moved his mouse and cleared his monitor.

"It isn't passworded," Chi said. "And he didn't have to make a phone call first." Her surprise showed in her voice.

"Or it doesn't come back to the password when it goes to a screen saver," David said. "He's the boss. Maybe he thinks that security rules are for underlings and don't apply to him. You'll have to come back here first thing in the morning and watch him when he first sits down at his desk. If there is a password, you need watch his fingers and memorize it. If not, we need to know that, too. For now, let's go back to the van and get the next name on the list."

David and Chi were able to investigate four floors before he had to return to do his exercises and eat his noon meal.

After the tray was pulled back under the door, David was surprised to see the guard pull aside the small curtain over the window in the door and ask, "Are you feeling OK, kid?"

"Why do you ask?" he responded.

"You look like crap," the guard responded. "It's bad enough I can see it in the cameras. And you aren't singing to yourself like you usually do."

"I get depressed in cloudy weather," David said truthfully. "This place is hell for me."– also truthful. He pointed over at the pipe in the ceiling. "If I couldn't see the sky through that pipe," he continued, "I would probably be pounding my head against the wall."

He paused a moment and then said, "It's starting to really get to me. Is there any way that I can get a little time outside?"

The guard looked genuinely concerned as he said, "I'm sorry, kid, I can't do that." He then smiled slightly and said, "Hang in there. I think this might all be over soon."

David felt anger flushing throughout his body but controlled himself. The guard obviously didn't know of the orders to kill him. He probably just knew that whatever was happening was happening soon. He forced his voice to sound calm as he answered, "That would be good."

A few minutes later, he was back standing under the pipe staring up into the mirror. This time he whispered, "Guard room" and appeared just outside his cell door.

The guard who had taken his tray was standing next to the other two guards who worked the same shift as he did. "Do you think the boss might let the kid go once everything is in place?" he asked.

The other guard answered curtly, "Ain't my problem. We just do what the boss orders." Then he added, "You goin' soft on the kid, Jake?"

"No," the first guard answered, "but he reminds

144

me a lot of my kid brother. I wouldn't want someone to treat Scott this way."

"He's not your brother," the third guard said, sounding angry. "You start thinkin' about prisoners as people, you can't do your job."

"But he is people," Jake replied. "And I'm worried about him."

David stood watching Jake for several minutes. He realized that he hadn't thought of his guards as people either. He'd seen their initials on the reports, but no names were ever written down and none of them had ever before called another by name. Now he knew the name of one of them and that made him a person. He wasn't a machine. He was a person who wanted to do the right thing... and his name was Jake.

A soft voice next to him asked, "What is wrong?"

He turned to see Chi standing next to him. "One of my guards asked if I was feeling OK," he answered. "His name is Jake. I think he really is concerned about me. He's actually not a bad person. He's just doing his job."

"We have nine more floors to investigate," Chi said firmly.

"Actually," David replied, "only seven. The first two floors are public shops and offices. There're no receptionist-guards for those floors."

"Then we need to go to Kiara, the receptionist-guard on the eighth floor," Chi replied. A moment later she shimmered and disappeared and David began saying softly, "Kiara, receptionist-guard, eighth floor."

Chapter Sixteen
"Reporting Back"

David and Chi continued their exploration of the Connors Building. Most of the offices seemed very ordinary. Despite having a receptionist-guard, the seventh floor turned out to be a purely mechanical floor dedicated to heat and power for the building. There were no offices on that floor. The sixth floor, one of the ones which was two-thirds used as a car park, was a huge server farm holding the massive Connors' super computers. Floors five, four, and three each housed a major subsidiary of Connors Armaments. Again there was nothing out of the ordinary in those offices so David and Chi decided to return to the computer floor.

On the sixth floor, behind the receptionist area, there was a very small office area separated by a glass wall from the computers. It was just large enough for two computer techs and a guard to have work cubicles. One of the techs appeared to be monitoring the various computer functions. The other seemed to be working on a program of some sort. The guard mainly sat nearly immobile at his desk playing some sort of game on his computer.

Twice while David and Chi were walking around, a phone buzzed at his desk. Without moving anything more than his hand, he flipped a switch on the front of the desk to answer the call through his headset. After looking carefully at the monitor in front of him, he entered a code into his keyboard and said, "You're connected." It looked like a really boring job, but the guard, who was grossly overweight, seemed ideally-suited to it.

"We have only a little time left before you lose the light for your mirror," Chi said. "We need to report back to Warrior Robert. They should be at the campground by now."

"There's nothing really to report," David said dejectedly.

"Are you forgetting," Chi replied, "that Mister Connors might have an open terminal on the network?"

"'Might' is the operative word," David said. "We won't know that until you come back in the morning."

Both then said "Van," shimmered, and disappeared.

When they arrived at the van, David stood watching as Chi shivered slightly and turned from the mirror. "David is here," she said to Momma Ling. Then, as Ling wrote furiously, she recited what they had seen– and not seen– at the Connors Building.

"Both of you," Kong Ling said firmly, "come out to the picnic table so you can hear what is discussed. Then both of you need to rest." She turned to where she thought David was standing near the mirror and said, "David, I assume that you look as exhausted as Kong Jing. I know time is running out, but you must rest when you can." After than she stuck her head out the side door of the van and called out, "He's here."

Once again, Robert, Lucy, and Ling sat on one side of the table. A folded blanket covered the bench on the other side. "I will summarize while David and Chi are here," Ling said. "We can discuss details later while they are resting."

After she said that, she looked over at the blanket with a face that showed her concern. "You do need to rest, my little Chi," she said softly. "I do not want to lose another daughter to the mirror."

Robert waited a moment and then said, "So what do you have?"

"Everything appears to be normal," Ling began. "Security is very tight in all offices, even the smaller offices of the subsidiary companies. There is a receptionist-guard on each floor except the ground floor and the first level above that. A key pad is needed to enter or leave the office area, itself. It opens the door and may or may not turn off alarms at night. The codes are automatically generated and are keyed to the year, day, hour, and minute... except they are offset by an amount that changes daily, or perhaps even more often.

"Frank Lufton uses a simple password for his computer, Operation TOP. Neither David nor Chi have any idea what it means. Jimmy was right about the computers, though, Frank has to call the guard on the sixth floor who connects him to the network, so the password is useless.

"Everett Connors' office takes up most of the twelfth floor– the top floor. It appears that he might be permanently connected to the network. While Chi and David were there he started work without calling the guard, so he might have an open connection. They do not know what his password is because his computer did not lock when it was not in use."

She glanced down at her notes for a while and then said, "The guards regularly check each floor from the elevator, but do not get out. They just check that the receptionist-guard gives the proper response."

She looked up a last time through her notes and said, "That is about it."

"Looks like it will be a lot easier if Connors actually does have a direct link," Robert said, "but either way we are going to have to get into that building and probably into the big man's office."

"And either way," Lucy added, "we are going to have to have Jimmy come down here and join us."

"Already here, cop lady," came a voice from the bushes and Jimmy stepped into the clearing. He startled slightly and held up his hands as Robert's Glock and Lucy's Berretta both suddenly appeared, pointed directly at him.

"How did you find us!?" Lucy demanded angrily.

He smiled broadly and said, "Like I said, cop lady, nothing is untraceable. I traced which satellite you were pinging off of. That got me to the Gulf coast. I figured you were headed for New Orleans because Connors is here, and guessed that you were camping to stay off the main grid."

He paused and smiled, "So I hacked into all the RV parks and looked for someone with a false ID."

"That ID is backstopped all the way up to the White House," Robert said defensively.

"Richard Blain doesn't pay any state taxes," Jimmy said with a smile. Then he added, "Neither does Walter Huft, Melodie Harris, and eleven others who are camped within thirty miles of New Orleans. Evidently there are a lot of crooks, spies, or tax dodgers hiding in New Orleans campgrounds."

He smiled again and said, "There were a lot to choose from, but I know that Detective Nash has a weakness for old movies."

He looked over at Robert and said, "That is why of all the campgrounds in all the towns in all the world, I walked in here."

Robert huffed, but said nothing. He and Lucy both made sure their weapons were safe and set them on the tabletop. As Jimmy started to sit down opposite them, Ling and Lucy loudly shouted "No!" in unison.

Jimmy jumped back to his feet and Robert said calmly, "David and Chi, I think you need to go rest. We will talk again tomorrow after Chi has checked out Mister Connors' morning sign on."

Ling walked the short distance back to the van and stuck her head in the door. She then walked back to the picnic table and sat down on the blanket. She gestured across from herself toward where she had been sitting and said, "You may be seated now, Jimmy."

Jimmy remained standing until Robert and Lucy put away their weapons and Robert also gestured for him to sit. Once he was seated, he said, "Either I'm taking some weird drugs, cop lady, or you have invisible friends."

"I guess we would have to explain this to him eventually," Robert said, looking at Lucy. "Should I or would it be best coming from you?"

"It would be best coming from me," Ling said very firmly. She then looked directly at Jimmy and said angrily, "But first I want to tell you this, young man. If you have endangered my little Chi by your reckless actions I will personally flay you alive."

Jimmy swallowed hard and said, "I don't know who Chi is, but I wouldn't endanger cop lady or anyone with her. No one followed me and my crew is absolutely loyal to me."

Looking at Lucy he asked softly, "Who is Chi?"

"Chi is my granddaughter," Ling answered, her voice still reflecting contained fury. "She is a Mirror-Walker, as is David Malone. They were both sitting here with us, or at least their mirror selves were. David is a captive of Mister Connors. Chi is asleep in the van. She is near exhaustion but will not stop going into the mirror until she has freed her teacher... or dies. She considers David to be a Master of the Mirror and she to be his student."

Jimmy looked over at Lucy and said softly, "What have you gotten me into, cop lady?"

"Jimmy," Lucy said evenly, "in all of those times you have been playing your games on line, have you ever been in a position where everyone is against you and the fate of the world depends upon what you do?"

Jimmy looked back at her in obvious confusion and said, "Couple of times, I guess. It gets pretty hairy when all the other players are after you."

"That is what is going on now, Jimmy," Lucy said. She reached over and put her hand on top of his. "Only this time, it isn't a game. Everett Connors wants to take the world to the brink of nuclear war and hold it there so he can make more money selling his bombs and bombers and everything else."

Ling spoke up, "Someone in my government, probably backed by munitions dealers or others who would profit from a new cold war, is also involved."

Jimmy looked over at Lucy and nodded his head at Ling. "She's not from around here, is she?" he asked.

Robert spoke up. "Kong Ling, I would like you to meet James 'Jimmy' O'Farrell of Plain City, Iowa. He is a genius in his own way and could be a quite successful person if he didn't spend all of his time trying to hack into anything with a vulnerability on the web. One of these days he's going to hack the wrong person and get arrested or whacked or hired as a White Hat for the government."

He then turned slightly so he was facing Jimmy and said, "Jimmy, I would like you to meet Kong Ling. She and her granddaughter Kong Jing, also known as Chi, are from Penglai, Shandong, China. Momma Ling has lost two children in the mirror and if you do anything that endangers Chi, I will personally sharpen the knife and then hold you down so she can skin you alive."

Ling smiled over at him and said, "My husband would have definitely enjoyed working with you, Detective Nash."

"I already plugged the holes in your Blain identity," Jimmy said quickly. "My RV is on the other side of the campground. It's got a full satellite link so I can work from here as easily as from home. Two of my most trusted friends are monitoring some primary nodes, screening for any mention of this campground or my name or the detective's or cop lady's. If anyone is looking for us, we'll know it before they can find us."

"I am sorry if I misjudged you," Ling said softly, "but we can trust no one in this."

Jimmy laughed softly and said, "Like I keep telling people, you aren't paranoid if there really are people out to get you."

He then turned to Robert and said, "What's the plan?"

"David and Chi have found a potential weakness in Connors' security," Robert began, "and it is old Everett himself. His terminal may be directly connected to the network and doesn't go through the guard for connection. We hope to get his passwords tomorrow morning. If we can get you into his office, you should be able to download everything we need."

"That's a big if, detective," Jimmy replied. "I've got the training manual for the guards. When those receptionist-guards leave for the day, they signal the main guard station and a motion detection alarm is turned on in that floor's lobby area. There is no way to disable it except at the main guard's desk. The keypad inside the office area opens the door and shuts off the alarms in the office area, but doesn't disable the alarm in the lobby. You have to call the guard's station and say you are leaving. Or if you are going up to one of the offices later at night, you have to tell the guard where you are going. They watch where the elevator is and acknowledge the alarm when you set it off. It resets after a real short time."

He shrugged his shoulders and said, "There is just no way to get in there without setting off the alarms."

Ling gave one of her half smiles and said, "Cousin Pelagia."

Robert, Lucy, and Jimmy all said, "What?" in

response.

"Cousin Pelagia is what you call an urban legend in the intelligence community," she explained. "Back when the Chinese were building a new embassy in Poland, the American CIA, of course, wanted to plant bugs throughout the building. We found all of them partially because we are so thorough at things like that, but also because the building was so far away from any other structure that the bugs had to be of higher power than usual. The Americans decided that if they could embed a repeater in one of the power poles which went past the embassy, they could use much lower-powered transmitters in their bugs and still receive their intelligence.

"The problem was how to hollow out one pole without it being obvious. They could not just climb up there and drill out the pole. And the poles were relatively new, so replacing one would stand out and be noticed. After months of effort and research by their engineers, they were about to give up when one of their low-level operators came up with a solution.

"Stefan Dabroski told his handler, 'Cousin Pelagia will do it for $250,000 American... guaranteed.' That was a lot of money in Poland in those days, but the Americans agreed and paid Stefan.

"Two days later, a petty criminal by the name of Pelagia Dabroski stole a delivery truck and took it for a joy ride. He careened down the street alongside the embassy grounds smashing fire hydrants, cars, and electric poles. He took out nearly a dozen poles on the road alongside the embassy. There were empty whisky bottles in the truck with him and he and his clothing reeked of liquor. He went to jail for two years. When he got out, his cousin Stefan gave him his half of the $250,000."

She smiled at Jimmy and said, "We did not find

out about the repeater until the power lines were buried years later. The pole broke as it was being taken down and the repeater transmitter was discovered."

Robert looked over at her and asked, "So, what would Cousin Pelagia do?"

"Set off all of the alarms in the building at once and enter while the guards are confused," she answered firmly.

"I can get you past the guards and up to the floor," Jimmy said. "Connors is going to be gone, so we don't have to worry about him being around. His pilot filed a flight plan for his plane, leaving tomorrow at noon. It was filed with an open destination. They sometimes do that just to be sure that they are in the queue for takeoff."

"And I know how to trigger the alarms," added Lucy. Turning toward Jimmy she added, "If you can hack into the heating system."

"Not a problem," answered Jimmy. He laughed slightly and said, "It's amazing how many places leave what they think are non-essential systems relatively unprotected."

"OK," Robert said. "All we need is the go from Chi. Nothing else we can do tonight. I'll drive out and bring us back some pizza." He paused and then said, "Yes, Jimmy, you can join us for supper."

"Thank you," Jimmy said. He then turned to Lucy and asked, "Would you like to see my RV, cop lady? I promise, nothing more than a tour."

Lucy looked over at Robert and then back to Jimmy before saying, "OK, but nothing more than a tour of your RV."

Chapter Seventeen
"Operation Hydra"

Ling woke Chi at five the next morning. "You can rest later today," she said as Chi groggily rose from her bed. "But we have to make sure you are already in the office before Mister Connors gets there."

Chi mumbled something as she walked over to the mirror. Despite the fact that the van was now sitting in the campground, she reached up and grabbed the ropes to help support her. She gave her grandmother a weak smile before turning to the mirror and saying, "The Evil One's office."

The office was empty when Chi arrived. While she was waiting, she wandered around the office. Except for the fact that it was exceptionally neat and tidy, there was nothing unusual about the office... except that painting of Hercules slaying the Hydra. She was still examining the painting when Mister Connors walked into the office.

He opened one of the tall doors behind his desk and put something inside, then he sat at his desk and moved his mouse. The screen immediately sprang to life. Chi watched carefully as he entered the password. She was afraid that she might not be able to remember the letters to give them to Warrior Robert, but Mister Connors sounded out the password as he entered it.

"Operation Hydra," he said firmly. "Nine years in the making. Derailed once by that young Houdini from Cornville, but now back on track and ready to roll."

He paused and said with a smile, "Three more days."

He typed the same password in a second time and the main menu for the Connors network appeared on his screen.

Chi was smiling in triumph as she turned from the

mirror and wrote the password on the notepad her grandmother had been using to brief the others.

A few minutes later, Ling was sitting with Robert, Lucy, and Jimmy at the picnic table. "Chi says the password is 'Operation Hydra,'– like the painting– with each word capitalized and an underline in place of the space." Ling began. "She also says that Mister Connors mumbled something about it happening in three days."

"Oh, my God!" Lucy said softly and began staring out into space.

"What!?" Robert said harshly.

"I think I know what they are planning," Lucy said. "Chi said there were two Senators at that dinner who were wearing the Peace Through Strength pins. Was Senator Harris one of them?"

Robert fumbled with a small notebook from his pocket. "Yes," he said, "I believe he was. Why is that important?"

"Senator Donald Harris is President Pro Tempore of the Senate," Lucy said. Her voice, as well as her body, was quivering. "If something happens to the President, Vice President, and Speaker of the House," she said firmly, "he is next in line to be President of the United States. Connors doesn't want to kill the Hydra. He wants to select which head will rule the snake."

Robert spoke slowly as he said, "They are going to do a mass assassination in three days."

He lay his small notebook on the table and began drawing his grid. He then sent a text message which read, "CX0LXL3A#" He was relying on the fact that as kids the 3X3 code square was the one they most often used and at one time either brother could decode it in his head. Translated, the message read, "CALLX#3X0."

As soon as the text was sent, Robert walked to the van and retrieved one of the satellite phones. It started ringing as he was sitting back down at the table. He answered it with, "Manure about to hit ventilator, little brother. Connors plans to assassinate top three and make Senator Harris President. Plan is for three days from now. Going in tonight. Look for data drop by midnight. If it isn't there, assume worst and get David out. Otherwise, call as soon as you have data."

The rest heard the "Acknowledged," as Robert was shutting off the phone.

"Impressive," Jimmy said. "Just under fifteen seconds. Not long enough to get a lock and a call that short isn't auto-recorded for later analysis."

"You seem to know an awful lot about how the NSA monitors electronic transmissions, young man," Robert said sternly. He then smiled and said, "Glad to have you on our team."

***

A little past three-thirty in the afternoon, a delivery van pulled up to the Connors office building. On the side, in big white letters, it said, "Our Business is Balloons." The background, which covered the entire rest of the van, was a jumble of brightly-colored balloons. There was also a small box which gave a telephone number and a website URL. OBB was a legitimate business in New Orleans. The driver, however, was the undercover agent Robert had met in Washington.

He opened the side door and took out a tray containing a dozen or more vases of flowers with bright Mylar balloons floating above each of them. On one side of the balloons was a big "Thank You," written in bright flowing script letters. Beneath it, written in a very nice script with a broad felt-tipped marker was a name. On the other side of the balloon it said, "National Receptionist Appreciation Day." Beneath that was tomorrow's date.

He walked up to the guard's desk in the main lobby and said, "I have a delivery for floors three through twelve."

"Who authorized this?" the guard said.

"We got an order from a Mister Everett Connors," the man replied, looking at a delivery slip he had pulled from his pocket. "He said it was time that the company recognized some of the little people."

The guard grunted slightly and said, "Maybe he should recognize the guard service sometime with a little pay increase." He then keyed his radio and said, "Jerry, got an escort for you."

A few minutes later, the elevator opened and another guard called out, "Escort."

"That's for you," the guard said and pointed to the delivery man and then the open elevator.

The escort guard stayed in the elevator while the delivery man stepped out at each floor and presented the receptionist with the balloon and flowers. Each of them was a highly-trained guard, but they were also women who were often taken for granted... and they knew it. The flowers would definitely stay on their desks until tomorrow proclaiming to everyone who passed that someone had finally noticed them.

***

Several people who had been planning to work late that night at the Connors Building decided to leave anyway. One complained that it just seemed so stuffy in their office area. He wasn't imagining things. Jimmy had shut down all of the air handlers at five-thirty. No ventilation was blowing anywhere in the building. By nine, several people had called the guard downstairs to complain. He told them there was nothing he could do until the maintenance people called him back. What he didn't know was that when he had called in the problem, Jimmy had re-directed the call. It was Lucy who had answered the phone and assured him that someone would be over as soon as possible.

Shortly before ten, Lucy, Jimmy, and Robert were walking up the alley toward the loading dock at the rear of the building. The security cameras for that area were part of the high security system, but the timers for the lights were on the low protection side. Robert checked the time and said softly, "Show time."

The lights blinked out and they hurried up onto the dock to the shipping office door. Its outer door was also on the low priority system. It popped open with a slight click when Robert twisted the handle. They had barely made it inside when the lights blinked back on.

"So far, so good," Robert muttered under his breath. They crossed the office and descended a set of stairs to a mechanical area in the basement. Jimmy's investigation said this area, for some reason, had no security cameras. Hopefully he was right.

The elevator buttons glowed dimly in the near darkness of the basement area. Robert pressed the call button and the three of them stood impatiently waiting. When the elevator doors finally opened, Robert stepped in, opened a small door, and quickly pressed a series of numbers on the control panel. A soft voice said, "Entering Maintenance Mode."

The guard at the night desk noted the elevator descending to the basement, but when he checked his logs he also noted that the elevator company had set a scheduled maintenance for tonight. When the elevator status disappeared from his monitor, he went back to playing a game on his phone. It didn't occur to him that no elevator personnel had checked in through his desk.

The elevator itself was no longer in the basement.

It was moving in maintenance mode to the top floor without signaling its position either at the floors or on the guard's monitor. They stopped at the twelfth floor. In maintenance mode, the doors would not open until the 'Open Door' button was pressed.

As they stood waiting, Lucy said, "Chi should be reporting back to Ling about now."

As if in answer, the satellite phone rang and Ling said quietly, "Chi says the clock inside the office is three minutes and thirty seconds faster than the one on the outside."

"Roger," Lucy said and turned to Jimmy who was looking at his own watch and silently counting down seconds. He held up his hand and said softly "Ten." Then he counted down, "Nine, eight, seven, six, five, four, three, two, one."

He smiled as they heard the squeak and squeal of every air handler in the building coming up to speed at the same time. The sudden onslaught of flowing air caused the balloons on the receptionist's desk on every floor to begin waving back and forth, triggering the motion sensors for that floor.

The three of them scurried across the entry lobby for the twelfth floor, pausing only for Lucy to hurriedly enter the proper code into the keypad. She smiled nervously as she quickly punched in the numbers, remembering to make the entry code three minutes and thirty seconds slower than the time displayed above the door. Once inside the office, Lucy again entered the code, this time moving the numbers three minutes and thirty seconds fast– the time above the door on the inside.

"The alarms should be off in here," Jimmy said. He looked at his watch and said, "Made it with nine seconds to spare." He pointed up at the vent above the door as the soft whine of the blower fans once again faded away.

Lucy opened the door to Everett's office and pointed at the desk. "Do your stuff, Jimmy," she said quietly.

Jimmy held up what looked like an oversized thumb drive and said, "Piece of cake, cop lady."

Robert and Lucy stood nervously at the door while Jimmy hummed and whistled to himself. About ten minutes later, he pulled the device back out of the computer and said with a smile, "I've got it all." He looked at his watch and said, "Train home leaves the depot in fourteen minutes."

While they were waiting, Jimmy asked Lucy, "How did you know this would work?"

She laughed. "When I was a rookie," she explained, "I was working night shift. We would get called over to City Hall real early just about every Friday morning. For some reason, the alarms would go off in the Mayor's office area at exactly four in the morning every time. We would check everything out and find nothing. Turns out that one of the city clerks was trying to put the moves on the Mayor's secretary. So, every Thursday night, he would wait until she had left and then put a bouquet of flowers on her desk with a floating balloon so she would find it in the morning. On the balloon, he would write his request that she go out with him that night.

"The heating system would go into night mode in that section at six. It never cooled off enough in there to call for heat until the system came out of night mode at four the next morning. The Mayor finally told her to go out with him or tell him to bring the flowers in the morning. ... They've been married for almost five years."

"I'll have to remember that one," Jimmy said.

After that, everyone quieted down and they all

stood waiting by the front door of the office until Jimmy once again began counting down to the restart of the air handlers. They could hear the alarms blaring throughout the building as they crossed back to the elevator and began their descent to the basement.

One the way down, Jimmy said, "I left them on this time. They will eventually figure out what caused the alarms to go off and put it down to a strange coincidence."

Actually, it took the guards over an hour to realize what was causing the alarms to trigger. The technician from the alarm company, who had been called to the scene, wanted them to throw the balloons away, but since the cards were signed by Mister Connors, they decided instead to merely put them where their movement would not be picked up by the motion sensors. When the receptionists came in the next morning, they found their flowers on the floor under their desks with their chairs trapping the balloons in place. A note in the center of each desk announced a new policy prohibiting any floating device being left in the lobbies overnight.

Chapter Eighteen
"The Taste of Freedom"

The next morning was almost impossible for David as he suffered through the minutes until he could stand beneath the vent pipe and go into the mirror. When the time finally came, Chi was standing by his side.

"It is time for you to leave here," she said softly. "Come, let me show you," she added and pulled him toward the guard room. She continued pulling until they passed through the outer door. Robert and Lucy were standing outside accompanied by a couple dozen armed soldiers. He could see his van in the parking area near the front of the bunker.

David turned to Chi and said, "Tell them to give me a minute to talk to the guards. We might be able to do this without violence."

Chi shimmered and disappeared. A few moments later, Ling stuck her head out of the door of the van and called for Robert. He spoke with her and then came back to where David was standing. "You have five minutes," he said firmly. "Then we come in."

Several of the soldiers looked around trying to see who Robert was speaking to.

David took a deep breath and looked down from the vent pipe. He walked over to the door of his cell and pounded on it hard, twice, with his fist. "Jake," he said softly, "we need to talk."

The curtain on the opening in the door was pulled back and Jake asked nervously, "How do you know my name?"

"More importantly," David said evenly, "I know that you are a person whom I don't want to see killed if it can be prevented."

"What do you mean?" one of the other guards said angrily.

163

"I mean that you have three minutes to put down your weapons and walk out with your hands in the air," David said.

"Or you'll what?" the guard rasped angrily.

"I won't do anything," David replied. "But if you do not surrender, in three minutes Seal Team Seven will blow the main door and come in firing. They know I am behind a thick wall and a steel door so they don't have to worry about me. Their primary orders are to rescue me alive and unharmed. Collateral damage has been authorized. If you do not surrender, you will die."

"Why should I believe you?" the guard snapped.

"Turn your beach cameras," David said.

The guard still sitting at the work table moved a toggle that should have panned the camera across the beach. He gasped and pointed at the screen. The image wasn't moving.

"They cut into your feeds and looped the image," David said softly. "Your radio communications are also blocked. Surrender or die."

The guard sitting at the desk stood up and yelled, "Don't shoot. We're coming out."

Before Jake left, he looked back in through the door window and said, "Thank you, David."

David said nothing in response. He couldn't. His body was shaking so severely that he had to sit down on the bed. The screech of the cell door being opened caused him to look up. Detective Nash and two members of the seal team were standing in front of him.

"Are you OK?" Robert asked.

"No," David said with a slight laugh, "but I will be as soon as I walk out of here."

"It's not over yet," Robert said. "We– and by we, I mean the President– we need you to talk to Frank Lufton."

"What does he want me to say?" David asked.

164

"I'll explain it on the helicopter ride back to New Orleans," Robert said. "Lucy will bring the van back and join us there later."

"Can Chi and Momma Ling ride with us?" David asked. "This may be our only chance to see each other in the flesh, so to speak."

"I think we can arrange that," Robert said. "But the Chinese want her back where they can protect her while all this blows over. A flight has already been arranged out of New Orleans."

"Protect or use?" David said bitterly.

"They probably wonder the same thing about us and you," Robert answered. "That's probably part of why they want Chi back on their soil. It keeps us in balance."

One of the flight crew from the helicopter was beckoning them. Robert trotted over to speak with him and then ambled back smiling. "The pilot says we have to leave now. They are supposed to drop Ling and Chi off at the airport to make their flight." He looked over at Kong Ling and Kong Jing who were hurrying toward them. "That means you have about forty-five minutes to sit and talk."

The only seats on the helicopter were along the sides and were more harnesses than seats. Several of the Seals pushed equipment satchels toward the rear of the area and motioned for David and Chi to be seated. Momma Ling sat alongside her granddaughter.

As they sat down, Chi looked up at Momma Ling and then said something in Chinese. Ling laughed slightly and David noticed that Chi appeared to blush. "She says that you look bigger with clothes on," Ling said with a smile.

"I was just thinking that she looked smaller," David answered. He also appeared to blush slightly.

David reached out his hand and lifted Chi's hair to

his face. "I will have to remember the smell and feel of her hair," he said softly. "There are almost no smells in the mirror and everything feels almost the same." He looked directly at Chi and said, "You have beautiful hair."

Ling was translating as David spoke. Chi leaned her face against David's hand. "She says that your hands are warm. She misses that in the mirror. Everything there is so cold."

David looked past Ling to where Robert was sitting on the floor. "We will never really be able to be together, will we?"

Tears came to Chi's eyes as her grandmother translated his words.

"Never is a long time," Robert replied. "And you will always have the mirror. It's more than some people get."

Chi snuggled her head against David's shoulder and began to cry softly. He reached up and stroked her head and then held her tight against his chest. They were still in their tight embrace when the helicopter landed near a military terminal at Louis Armstrong Airport. A small contingent of Chinese diplomats was awaiting them.

As Kong Ling stepped down from the 'copter, she turned and spoke to David. "I will protect my little Chi as much as I can in this world," she said firmly, "but you are her teacher and her master. You are the one who must protect her in the mirror world."

"I will always," David said. He started to say something else, but several of the Chinese waiting on the ground began speaking at once. He tried to smile as he watched Kong Ling and Chi get into the limousine, but he could feel the tears spilling down his face.

Chapter Nineteen
"Negotiations at the Highest Level"

A little over an hour later David, Robert, and twenty-nine members of Seal Team Seven walked into the lobby of the Connors Armaments building. "I need the master key for the elevator," David said as he walked up to desk.

"I'm sorry," the guard replied, "but I can't..." his words stopped there as a half dozen weapons clacked to ready and pointed at him.

"Do we need to tell you not to try anything?" Robert asked sharply.

"No, sir," the guard answered as he sat back down and placed his hands on the desk in front of him. "All keys are in the top right-hand drawer."

When the elevator doors opened on the ninth floor, the receptionist-guard reacted immediately, reaching beneath her desk to where a weapon was mounted, ready for use. She stopped, however, when five red dots suddenly showed on her chest. "The sixth weapon is aimed at your forehead," one of the Seals said firmly.

The guard slowly pulled her hands back to where they could be seen and placed them palms down on the desk in front of her.

"Please tell Mister Lufton that David Malone is here to see him," David said with a slight smile. "Also tell him not to do anything stupid until he has talked to me." He paused and then said, "You might mention that the rest of Seal Team Seven is downstairs in the lobby. And that a Delta Force Team is on the roof."

The receptionist-guard very deliberately reached for her phone and pressed two numbers on the keypad. "Frank," she said, "a David Malone is here to see you. Seal Team Seven is with him. He says not to do anything until you have talked to him. He also says that a Delta Force Team is on the roof."

There was silence for several seconds and then a deep voice said, "Send him in."

David walked over to the door and then turned to the receptionist-guard and asked, "What is the offset today?"

"Plus one forty-five," she answered automatically and then stared at him in amazement as he entered the proper code to enter the office.

Frank Lufton was sitting behind his desk as David entered the room. "So," he said, "you got away."

"Yup," David replied. "I got away."

"How'd you do it?" Frank asked calmly.

"You should have done a complete inspection of my cell when the guards told you I had stopped singing," David replied.

"Where was the mirror?" Frank asked.

"In the vent pipe," David answered. "Another Mirror-Walker found me and they put a mirror where I could see it in the pipe."

"The Chinese chick?" he asked.

"Her name is Kong Jing," David replied angrily. "And you tried to kill her!"

"That wasn't me!" Frank bristled. "The boss brought in an independent contractor without consulting me. I told him it was a mistake– especially to do something that public. He ignored me and made a second attempt without telling me."

He huffed out a short exhalation of breath before saying, "The morons he hired botched it twice with collateral damage both times.

"If it had been me or my men," he said firmly, "there would have been no public fuss and you would have had a cellmate at the Fort."

"Someone wants to talk to you," David said, setting a rather large laptop computer on the desk.

"Who?"

"See for yourself," David said as he opened the laptop with the monitor facing away from himself. "He's coming in through your boss' personal microwave link... and a couple of repeaters the Delta Force lowered down the elevator shafts."

Frank Lufton's eyes widened as he realized who was looking at him from the monitor. For a man like him, that was the equivalent of a violent scream.

A voice came from the laptop speakers. "Mister Lufton, I want to talk to you this morning, not as a President whom you tried to assassinate, but rather as a businessman who wishes to negotiate."

"I'm not sure what you mean, Mister President," Frank said softly.

"You are a mercenary, Mister Lufton... a good one... a very good one," the President said. "In the world in which we currently live, there are some things which cannot be done directly by a government." He paused. "And good mercenaries are hard to find."

The two men looked intently at each other silently, sizing each other up as if they were sitting in the same room. After a short while, the President broke the silence. "It would seem," he began, "that once again I have a question which I have to answer: 'Mister Lufton, do I use you as an asset or neutralize you as a threat?'"

"What guarantee do I have," Frank replied warily, "that once you have used me you won't neutralize me anyway?"

"None," Douglas Travis said with a laugh. "None at all. But as I said, good mercenaries are hard to find. If we can establish an... exclusive... contract for your services, I will not be the one to break that contract."

"What do you want done?" Frank asked.

"I have someone who must be neutralized without anyone ever knowing that it has been done. I don't mean

169

that they disappear or die or anything like that. I mean that their power is removed and they are made insignificant without anyone ever suspecting that anything has been done. A competitor of yours is being given a similar task in China, but I think in that case, less finesse is acceptable. I believe a plane crash is being arranged."

"I assume," Frank continued, "that this person is well-guarded and well-protected."

"He has," the President replied, "the best armaments in the world at his disposal, and he rides around in a car that is better protected than my own... which he built."

Frank chuckled slightly. "I'm sure that he has thought of every possibility," he said. "I will have to really think outside the box to pull this off."

"Perhaps Cousin Pelagia will think of something," David said from behind the laptop.

Frank looked up and him and raised his eyebrows. "I greatly underestimated you and your friends, young man," he said slowly. "No one told me you were so closely-connected to the spook shops."

"Who's Cousin Pelagia?" the President asked.

"It's an inside joke," Frank answered, "among people who work in the shadows. He is someone who does the impossible in a very simple way. No one knows if the story is true, but it reminds those of us in our line of work that sometimes the simplest way is the most effective."

Chapter Twenty
"Accidents Will Happen"

Ostensibly, Everett Connors was in Washington to testify before a congressional committee. That was partly true, but the whole truth was that he was in Washington because he wanted to be there– or at least nearby– when coordinated, ultra-long-range sniper attacks took down the President, Vice President, Speaker of the House, and President Pro Tempore of the Senate. That last attack would be unsuccessful. The bullet would instead strike Senator Harris' wife, who was standing alongside him. Some men are bought with money. Other's sell themselves even less honorably.

Everett could be sure of successful kill shots because the snipers would be using the smart rifles and smart bullets which his company had developed. The sniper pinpointed the target in the special scope, but it was a special computer which guided the bullet on its two-mile path to its target. Like the miniature missile that it actually was, the bullet carried a high-density explosive which would cause massive physical damage on impact. The intended target area was high on the torso near the neck, where protective armor would be the weakest. The result would be instant death, perhaps even total decapitation.

He could be sure all of the targets would be in the open at the same time because no politician could risk not observing Memorial Day in some fashion that would appear properly on the evening news. The President would be laying a wreath at the Tomb of the Unknown Soldier at Arlington Cemetery. The Speaker of the House, who had recently pushed through legislation for needed repairs and maintenance at the Tomb would also be present. The Vice President, whose grandfather died in World War II, would be at a similar ceremony occurring at the same time at the WWII memorial at the Mall. Senator Harris would be in his home state of Vermont, dedicating a new memorial to all of the women who have died in defense of their country. It would be an ironic twist of fate that his wife would die at the base of that memorial.

Security forces would respond immediately, and the snipers would die in a hail of gunfire. They didn't know that, of course. They never do. Paid assassins always assume that you will be honorable and live up to your end of the contract. Only fanatics and heroes intentionally embark on suicide missions.

The set-up for the sniper at the WWII memorial was relatively simple. There are, after all, many places around the Mall that a van can be placed unobtrusively on such an occasion. That is especially true if it has a large satellite dish on its roof and the emblem of a major news network on its side. Getting a sniper in place at Arlington National Cemetery was a little more difficult– and expensive– to set up.

A movie honoring a fictitious American hero was being filmed in the Washington area. The director, somehow, had received permission to shoot a burial scene on Memorial Day. Their argument was that they wanted the cemetery to appear as it naturally would on that day. After a great deal of discussion– and pressure from several Senators and Congressmen– the filming was allowed. The filming could not distract from the laying of the wreath, but the mock funeral procession with a caisson carrying a flag-draped casket would be allowed to form on a hillside some distance from the Tomb. The fact that the casket was slightly longer than normal would not be noticed. With the additional length, only an inch or two of the barrel had to extend from the end of the casket. The shots themselves would not be heard more than a few feet from the caisson and those who heard them would think that they were part of an honor salute somewhere in the cemetery.

What Mister Connors did not know was that the fake casket would now be empty. And the fake news van would be nowhere to be seen. And Vivian Harris would come home from the dedication to find an envelope filled with proof of her husband's infidelity sitting on the vanity in her bedroom.

Frank Lufton had arranged for the snipers. He had personally given the original orders. A simple, verifiable message from him saying, "Plans changed. Operation compromised. Payment in full. Stand down," was all that was needed.

Everett Connors was blissfully unaware that he had become the target that day. He was riding in his special armored limousine to Reagan International Airport when an armored truck like those normally used to carry large shipments of money ran a red light and struck his limo.

The two extremely heavy vehicles seemed to be fused together by the force of the impact, but the limousine– a newer model than even the President's– appeared to be intact. When the limousine came to a stop, however, Mister Connors was unconscious in the back seat.

When he came to, he was lying on a cot in a dim cell with concrete walls. It looked old. Green paint was peeling from the concrete. What light came through narrow slits at the top of the walls reflected strangely in the room. He shakily pulled himself to his feet, but before he could investigate his surroundings, a voice from behind him said cordially, "Welcome to Battery Langdon, Mister Connors."

He jumped up and spun toward the source of the voice. A young man was standing next to the doorway. "My name is David Malone," he said. "You are going to be here for a little while."

"My people will find me," Everett said defiantly.

"Your people," David replied, "think you suffered a severe head injury when your limo was T-boned by a bank truck. You were unconscious when you were taken to the hospital. The prognosis is not good. You are going to have a lot of memory problems when you finally get out. Then you are going to start acting very strangely in public. It will soon be obvious that you have brain damage. You become so paranoid and delusional that you will have become a threat to yourself and others... and especially to your business."

David motioned for Mister Connors to be seated, but he refused and David continued, "Your board of directors will have you declared incompetent. You will again be hospitalized. The best doctors and medications will be to no avail. For your own best interests, you will be confined to your estate in the mountains where you will live out the remainder of your natural life cut off from the rest of the world."

David looked at him impassively and finished with, "At that point, the real you will leave here and replace the actor who is playing your part until you return."

"You're that mirror boy!" Connors said angrily.

"Yes, I am," David replied in a matter of fact tone. He then pointed to several large mirrors which were mounted on the walls– and even the ceiling– of the cell. "Chi and I... and the others... will be keeping an eye on you from now on."

"This charade will not work," Connors said. "Once I am back I will tell people what you have done to me."

David smiled at him. "You do that," he said, almost viciously. "You tell people that you weren't really injured in the accident despite what all the expert doctors have said. Two people who walk in mirrors

174

coordinated the timing so that the truck could strike your ultimate limo in just the right place and penetrate your armor in a weak point with a thin metal spike. A fast-acting gas was then pumped into the limo through that spike rendering you unconscious. You were taken to an old, abandoned bunker on the beach for the summer where the mirror people watched over you and mercenary ex-Marine Corps guards made sure you didn't escape. Then, on the ambulance ride from the hospital to your place in the mountains, you were magically switched back.

"You can then tell them that you are now back in your own world, but the mirror people still watch you from every shiny surface around you. And long-range black ops snipers equipped with your magic missile bullets hide in the woods waiting for you to show yourself outside your house."

David laughed again as he said quickly. "You tell them that..." His voice suddenly turned very angry and very loud as he yelled out, "... and see if they believe you!"

He stood breathing heavily for a moment apparently trying to control his anger. Then he said firmly. "I could almost accept what you did to me. You got me out of the way so I couldn't mess up your plans."

His voice again rose to a yell as he finished with, "But you tried to kill Chi! I will never forgive you for that!"

David turned and walked out of the room. As he did, a burly guard in a Marine uniform stepped in. "In case you have any thoughts of overpowering me and escaping," he said politely. "I'm the only one on this detail who doesn't have orders to shoot you on sight."

Everett Connors sat back on the small bed and buried his face in his hands.

Epilogue
"A Return to Normal"

The movie was already playing on the television in the living room when David called out from the bedroom, "I'm almost ready, Chi. I'll be out in a moment."

He checked the alarm panel to be sure that everything was set to Protection Mode and activated. He also checked that the heavy steel door between the bedroom and the office was closed and the deadbolts were locked. He glanced over at the windows. The retractable bars were rolled down and in place.

"You aren't paranoid if there really are people out to get you," he said softly to himself as he dropped his robe on the bed and turned to face the mirror. He had learned that as a master of the mirror, all he really needed was enough mirror to show the opening to his soul. But he had also learned that entering and staying in the mirror that way took a tremendous amount of energy.

A moment later he appeared in the living room beside Chi.

"We do not have to watch this particular movie," she said as he appeared.

"Yes, we do," he answered softly, "or at least, I do. I need to return to my life before this all began."

"No man ever steps in the same river twice," Chi replied. "for it is not the same river and he is not the same man."

"Confucius?" David asked.

"Grandfather said it was a Greek philosopher," Chi answered. "I think the name was Heraclitus."

She smiled and said, "But Confucius probably said something very similar... because it is the truth. We can never go back to what once was."

"I know," David said softly. "But now I also know

176

why Chou would go back to the site of your ancestral village." He paused as she looked at Chi. "He knew the village was gone and would never be again," he said, "but it was a place where he could remember what was."

"And what might have been," added Chi.

David looked around him and said, "We are back here in my living room. It's not the same as it was when they broke in and took me. And we are not the same. But for now, we are here."

He leaned over and gave Chi a gentle kiss on the lips and then snuggled beside her to watch the rest of the movie that had been interrupted so violently so many weeks before.

THE END